CHRIS R

GW00728886

YOU
DON'T
SEE
ME

Little
Island
Books create waves

YOU DON'T SEE ME

First published in 2024 by
Little Island Books
7 Kenilworth Park
Dublin 6w
Ireland

First published in the USA by Little Island in 2025

A British Library Cataloguing in Publication record for this
book is available from the British Library.

Cover design by Jo Walker
Typesetting by Rosa Devine
Proofread by Emma Dunne
Printed in Poland by L&C

Print ISBN: 9781915071552

Little Island has received funding to support this book from
the Arts Council of Ireland/An Chomhairle Ealaíon

10 9 8 7 6 5 4 3 2 1

AUTHOR'S NOTE

Since childhood, writing has helped me escape from the confines of my life as a trans person. In words I can escape from reality. In words I can also introduce people to the lives of those often misrepresented or misunderstood.

In this book, I wanted to show the everyday emotions of being a transgender teenager, a story very personal to me. I framed it in a love story, as trans people are no different from anyone else – they want to feel loved and accepted for who they are. However, for a trans person, this comes with many difficult complications.

Ros, the main character, is a version of me, and I am grateful to Little Island for their support and encouragement in giving Ros a voice. Hopefully, this book will help trans people on their journey, and help others to gain more understanding of trans people's everyday issues.

— Chris Ricketts, April 2024

For those brave enough to be themselves, I salute you.

When a man rightly sees his soul,
He sees no death, no sickness or distress.
When a man rightly sees,
He sees all, he wins all
Completely.

Verse 7.26.2 Chandoga Upanisad
From Mr Cunningham's RE class

Are we our bodies, or are we much more?
I hope for my sake it's more.
I hate my body
But maybe one day that will change.

Ros Hughes, age 17

I don't know what to write. For the first time, I am lost for words. They usually flow, but now they're abandoning me. I can't leave the page empty with just a title. So I write the lyrics of her song.

The first time I met you I knew you were the one,
I held you in my arms and my life truly begun,
We laughed and we danced, and sang listening to rain,
And I never want to be without you again.
Dance with me, dance with me,
Let me be the one.
Dance with me, dance with me,
Until the day is done.

Maybe that's the way to avoid feeling empty. Maybe to avoid pain would be to dance with Eddy for ever.

PART ONE
A Constructed Reality

3.20pm
Thursday
Religious education class

You'd have to feel sorry for Mr Cunningham. Transition years are not interested in world religions at the best of times, but, last class of the day, everyone is tired and just wants to go home. He is a resilient man, though. He refuses to give up on the challenge of 4B and resort to a video. I wish he would. Maybe another Ted Talk on resilience – the quality we teenagers are accused of not having these days. We are the children of snowflakes, sad teenagers who will thaw too easily, given a roasting by anything or anyone in life.

'Dukkha.' He scribbles the word on his laptop as he talks. His scrawl appears on the whiteboard. 'It means all life is suffering.'

'Like being in this class, sir!'

'Very funny, Carl. Would you like to guess how much suffering I can put you through for being cheeky?'

A whoop of derision rises around the class. Mr Cunningham ignores them and sails straight into his elaboration of 'dukkha'.

'It means the suffering we go through in everyday life – the pain, grief and misery – but there is hope of release from this suffering.'

'It's called four o'clock,' another voice mutters.

There is muffled laughter, but again Mr Cunningham remains calm. I like him for that. Some teachers lose the plot at the smallest transgressions. It's usually the same five or six boys who try to irritate them. Morrissey's crew. Tadhg Morrissey is an arse. My mum would be furious at me for using such an unladylike word. But that is precisely why I use it.

That's Tadhg Morrissey, second row from the back with the shirt collar turned up and his tie undone. He rarely behaves in class and is in a constant state of detention. He has run out of Wednesdays in which to complete his punishments, but he doesn't give a damn. That's down to the principal, Mr Whelan. He's mad about rugby and Tadhg is out-half for the school team so he's always given special dispensation to play. He also has a face the Flock adore. God, I could write a whole book about them. They are found in the corner of every classroom, filing their nails or trying to become famous with another stupid TikTok.

That's the Flock. The girls at the back of the class on the left. Girls who, the consensus is, are the best-looking among the female contingent. Hair and make-up flirting with the edge of the permissible, they talk in whispers, eyeing the boys with either suspicion or giggles. Huddled around the one radiator, there is always one of them anorexic or bulimic. Boys only like super-skinny girls according to them. So the Flock wear their anorexia like a badge of honour. That's serious, I know, and we are supposed to report any eating disorders we notice to Ms McGlynn, but we never do. There would be too many to report. And then most of us don't really give a damn about what is happening in each other's lives. We have enough problems of our own. The clever bunch *pretend* to care. They sit there with their perfect uniforms and look devastated at the mention of any suffering – starving babies, refugees, people caught up in war. But most of us don't have enough space in our sympathy lockers to cram in another suffering human. Or maybe that's just me?

'So we escape dukkha by knowing the atman,' Mr Cunningham continues.

'Is that the dude in the Nintendo game, sir?' Carl Flynn just doesn't know when to give up. He is dying to become part of Morrisey's crew. It's sad to watch him playing to the audience, looking for acceptance. He will never fit in, though. He just isn't cool enough. It's the way his hair sticks up, his teeth are shackled by braces and his eagerness leaves him open to derision. If Carl was in a litter, he would have been the one left to die.

I can't wait for the end of class. The sound of the bell echoing through the building, the doors suddenly opening out on to the corridor. We become wild animals streaming away from our predators, rushing to be free. I am so lost in my thoughts that I don't realise a predator is circling and about to attack.

'Rosalyn, have you left the building already? I asked you what the word "atman" means?'

I hadn't noticed Mr Cunningham moving from behind his desk. But now I can smell the canteen lasagne he has eaten for lunch as he looms over me.

'Sorry, sir, I didn't catch what you said.'

'If we can escape from suffering by knowing our atman, what could it be, Rosalyn?'

Oh, god, go away. Do I care about your bloody subject? My whole life is suffering. I have periodic acne, my body has changed so much that it is alien to me, and my parents still think that I want to go for family outings to the local woods to forage for edible mushrooms.

'I don't know, sir.'

'Well, would you like to guess? Teachers are not supposed to spoon-feed students these days. We're supposed to challenge you to think for yourselves. So let's make an effort, shall we?'

Effort. He wants an effort. That's what happens every day when I get out of bed. It is an effort to attend school, especially for 'Transition Year' – that 'enlightened' non-year we have to do between one exam cycle and the next. Some of us don't want to explore who we are for a whole year. We just want to finish school, get the piece of paper that ends our education, and move forward to the next hamster wheel.

I give Mr Cunningham a blank look. I need him to go away. I don't need to be the centre of attention. The Flock has stopped filing their nails and passing notes and are now focused on me. I can feel the palms of my hands starting to sweat.

Mr Cunningham gives a wry smile and turns back to the whiteboard. Why has he let me off the hook?

'We are going to go around the class and every one of you can give me your idea of what atman might be. And you had better make your answers reasonable. Remember, the clue is that knowing atman can release you from the suffering we go through in life.'

Eamonn Walters, our resident goth, is happy to play the game. His hand shoots up. 'Atman must be the grim reaper himself, Mr Cunningham. Because dying would release us from suffering. Kurt Cobain knew what he was doing.'

There is a murmur of anticipation around the class. We all know what is going to happen next. It is like watching a car crash and seeing the victim shoot out through the windscreen. Mr Cunningham is already lying in the centre of the road, waiting to be run over by the juggernaut that is the topic of suicide. A topic we know every teacher avoids like the plague. Can he pick himself up from the tarmac and save himself, or will he be crushed?

'Death is a good answer, Eamonn. As when we die, we do go to heaven – or nirvana, of course, if we're a Hindu.'

Oops. A mistake mentioning nirvana.

'Do you think that's why Cobain called his band Nirvana, Mr Cunningham? Do you think he always wanted to escape this life?'

Eamonn is now driving the juggernaut mercilessly over the defenceless Mr Cunningham. We can sense he is bleeding out. We can see the beads of sweat on his forehead. Can he extricate himself from this mess before the class finishes?

'Atman is not death,' he announces, deciding to lift himself up from the ground with a strong statement of fact. 'Atman means "soul". Knowing our soul relieves us from the sufferings of this life.'

The bell can't come quickly enough for Mr Cunningham. It goes off at 3.55 precisely. Mr Cunningham is breathing a sigh of relief. No-one waits for the class to be dismissed. The chairs scrape back on the polished floor and the chatter begins, as we all exchange information about whether we are going to afternoon sport or not.

'Please put your chairs on your desks and any paper on the floor in the bin.'

Mr Cunningham can hardly be heard above the ascending noise, but most of us obediently follow his instructions. It is automatic by the time you reach TY. Four years of the same request see nearly all the chairs placed on desks. There are always a few casualties from swinging backpacks as we squeeze past each other to get to the door.

A wind is circulating the hockey pitches and the coach seems to feel a few more laps than usual would be beneficial.

'Come on, let's get moving. Back to the front, let's go!'

I hate running laps. But most of all, I hate doing the 'last man from the back' sprints. I always find it so hard to reach the front of the line. I'm just not fast. I'm built more for power than speed. I like that about my physique. I like being the strongest on the team. I don't even mind the nickname my team have given me. In fact, I encourage it.

'Here comes the Beast. Watch your backs.' The coach never stops this ribbing. He reckons it's friendly banter and he's happy when I'm drilling the ball through the opposition.

'Great saves today, Rosalyn!'

No matter how many times I ask to be called Ros, teachers keep lapsing back to the name on their roll sheet.

'Just give Jessica the heads-up before you drill it towards her.'

'Of course, coach.'

'Good girl. Not many goalies have your power or accuracy. You nearly took her ankle off.'

But he has lost me at 'good girl'. I hate that. I hate being called a 'good girl'. Mr O'Brien is probably wondering why I am glaring at him. I want to tell him exactly how I feel, but I know he won't get it. I know no-one will. Why would they? Sometimes *I* don't get me, and I definitely don't want to *be* me.

'You were great out there today, Ros. You're so brave throwing yourself down in front of the ball. I couldn't do it.' Sarah Bradshaw, my best and oldest friend, holds out a bottle of water. 'Are you going to Tadhg's house tonight? Seemingly there'll be alcohol,' she says.

'I don't know. I haven't finished my history project.'

'Don't be so boring, Ros. The whole team is going, and we need to bring the Beast. It won't be fun otherwise. Come with us.'

'Maybe.'

'Not maybe. Definitely. I will text you later, and we can go together. I hate arriving at a party on my own.'

'OK, message me and I might.'

6.30pm
Thursday
27 Beechfield Drive

'Rosalyn, dinner will be ready soon. Come downstairs and bring Ian with you.'

It is pitch black outside. It has been miserably wet and dark since half-way through hockey training. I hate winter evenings. For me that's dukkha. I write the word down in my journal. It contains all my thoughts but never my emotions. I don't like being emotional. I prefer being analytical, calm and in control. But in truth, I am just burying my emotions. Bit by bit I am putting them into boxes and storing them away in the recesses of my mind, like the Ark of the Covenant in the old Indiana Jones film. In fact, my mind looks exactly like that cavernous storage space. Nothing is out in the open. Everything is hidden.

I scribble the word 'duhkha' into my journal for a second time, doubling my sense of suffering.

Dukkha. Now that's a word I understand. And how am I not meant to suffer? I hate myself. I wish I was Tadhg with his confidence or even my brother. Life is so certain for them. Everything mapped out. Ian has a girlfriend, a college course that will give him a good career, and the hope of one day being something. Whereas I am a nobody, except on the hockey pitch. I would be the Beast twenty-four hours a day if I could. Or maybe I could just escape Beechfield Drive and find a way of being the real me.

I read back over my words. I have always wondered if I have some weird brain condition. I can't use shortened words, bad language or miss out on punctuation, even in my journal. I have to be in control of everything that comes from my pen. Maybe it is the same condition that makes me arrange all my T-shirts in the wardrobe in coloured groups. Maybe I have OCD. We learned about it in wellbeing class a few months ago. A condition born out of the need to be in control of something insignificant, when everything significant is out of your hands, and life is a mess you can't control.

Wellbeing is a class with Ms Spencer – 'but call me Daisy, lads, as we're all young here'. She doesn't look much older than us. She is barely one and a half metres tall, with shoulder-length blond hair and a cute Northern Irish accent. She says 'surely' in nearly every sentence. So the boys call her 'Shirley Spencer' behind her back. It is always the youngest teachers in the school who take wellbeing, as if their being closer to our age might help us divulge all our teenage angst and issues to them. I hate the class. It's a nightmare of a subject, all touchy-feely crap. And poor Shirley is just like the rest of the young well-being teachers, enthusiastic for the first few weeks and then, when nobody talks back, they resort to the obvious heartfelt videos, most of them Ted Talks. Recently, we had a video on a double amputee who had taken part in the Olympics, which was supposed to help all of us see how lucky we are, even when our acne is flaring. Does it hell!

'Rosalyn, did you hear me? Get your brother down from his room and come for dinner. It will be on the table in a minute.'

I open my desk drawer and hide the journal under the magazines. Nobody can ever read this – my life would be over. Yes, I am a typical teenager, prone to emotional exaggeration.

Dinnertime is always a report of the day, looking for anything to get mildly excited about.

'How did college go today, Ian?'

'Same as usual.'

'Good, glad to hear it. And do you have a match this weekend?'

Ian is always more animated when discussing rugby.

'Two o'clock against Trinity. Can I borrow the car? I said I would pick up some of the lads, if that's OK?'

My father always acquiesces. He can't say no to Ian. Captain of the under-21s team. Dad sees him as destined for great things and basks in the warmth of that coming glory. He imagines sitting in the Aviva stadium with a plastic pint in his hand, reading Ian's name in the match-day programme.

'Of course, take your mother's car. I might drop up to watch your match, if I get my round finished on time.'

The 'round' is golf with his mates from work. I don't think dad ever wins but he diligently tries every Saturday.

My mum smiles. 'Of course you can take the Mini, love. Just try not to let your friends wear their rugby boots in the car. There was mud left all over it a few weeks ago.'

Ian nods and then they exchange one of those looks that only seem to happen between mothers and their sons – a look of which Narcissus would have been proud.

Then it's me in the spotlight. Briefly.

'How about you, Rosalyn, do you have a match this weekend?'

'Yeah, ten o'clock against Muckross.'

There is no response to my announcement. Another conversation has started between my father and Ian over whether the next James Bond should be a woman or not.

'No woman can play James Bond,' my mother interjects. 'Surely she would have to be Jemima Bond in that case.'

There is a chorus of groans around the table.

'Don't trivialise it, Mum, the real question is whether a woman can be a spy with the number 007,' Ian says, 'not the character James Bond himself.'

'I think a woman could play James Bond,' I say.

Ian and Dad look at me askance.

'Come on, Ros, don't be controversial for the sake of it.'

'I'm not, Ian. Maybe it's time to take gender stereotypes off our screens and make characters like Bond more diversified.'

'Jesus, Rosalyn, have you been listening in wellbeing class again?' Ian laughs. 'For god's sake, we don't need to change everything in life to fit into the new diverse future. You'll want a drag queen playing Bond next. We should still allow heteronormativity and cis to exist on our screens.'

My mother and father look at each other.

'What are they talking about, Colin?'

'Damned if I know. It might be easier to get back to talking matches at the weekend.'

8pm
Thursday
The Lodge (Tadhg's house)

The driveway is full of teenagers, smoking cigarettes and drinking bottles of beer. Tadhg's parents have installed outside heaters. They hope it will deter the smokers among us from burning holes in their Persian carpets. They have a lot of money, but few parenting skills, and that's my opinion as a teenager, so god knows what other parents make of them. I haven't told my parents exactly where I am. I thought better of it. But they did grill me on the details of my evening out.

'So, what's this girls' night about? After all you have school tomorrow, Rosalyn.'

'It's just a small party for Anne-Marie's sixteenth.'

'Do we know Anne-Marie?'

'No, she's the new American girl, over with her family for a year. I think they're Pentecostalists, or something religious like that, so it's just a film and popcorn in her house.'

We had learned about the Pentecostal faith three weeks ago. I thought it was a convincing touch to my story. I didn't like lying to my parents, but then I lied every day about far more important things, so the little lies were easier to tell. They seemed insignificant compared to the major deceit.

'Sarah's going too. We won't be late, and her dad said he'd bring me home.'

Once you tell one lie then you're always stuck telling another.

'That's good. I have my writing club tonight. Tell Bill thank you for me.'

'Of course.'

So now I am here at a party which is far from any innocent Pentecostal gathering.

Sarah is elbowing me gently.

'Look who's arrived, Ros.'

Paddy Fitzpatrick is walking up the driveway in a leather jacket. All Tadhg's crew turn to greet him. He is a legend in their eyes. Suspended from school for sticking to his principles. Boys aren't allowed long hair or earrings. He came to school with both. He refused to get his hair cut when the year head told him it was short hair or suspension. He refused on the grounds that it was an unfair school rule. Girls could have short hair so why could boys not have long hair? Girls could have a pair of stud earrings so why could boys not have the same? Paddy put a petition online to send to the board of governors to express his opinion on the subject. No-one had done that before. Everyone had said that you could tell he was the son of a left-wing politician.

'Do you think his petition will work?'

'God, no. Why would it, Ros? Everyone knows Mr Whelan is old-fashioned. And he's a principal who doesn't go back on what he says. Anyway, I don't think Paddy wants to come back.'

'What do you mean?'

'Says he's leaving school after TY. He's going down the country somewhere.'

'Why?'

Sarah shakes her head. 'To be honest, I haven't a clue. I wasn't really interested. He's dope, but he's also a bit too strange.'

I look towards Paddy. Some of the Flock are now leaning against the wall where he is standing, adopting a variety of poses. I try to look at him through their eyes. Is he good-looking? His hair is perfectly brushed, and I'm sure he is wearing eyeliner – either that or he has the most startling eyes. He also has designer stubble, which has appeared since his suspension. Only boys in fifth and sixth years are allowed facial hair. It is probably part of his petition too. Facial hair for everybody.

'Do you want another beer, Ros?' Sarah asks.

'I didn't even want the first one.'

'Well, I did offer you vodka.'

'It makes me puke!'

'So that's even better! You can't get fat when you're puking.'

'Jesus, Sarah, you shouldn't care about that.'

'That's all right for you to say. You're the Beast. You're expected to be strong and ...'

'And what? Go ahead, say it. Are you searching for the word "fat"?'

'Duh, don't be so sensitive. You're not fat, you're just built. It's who you are, Ros. You're not a girly girl and you know it. And I'm sure you don't want to be like the Flock either.'

'What's that meant to mean, Sarah?'

My mood isn't good, so I decide to escape before I become more of a douchebag. 'I'm going to find a toilet. Why don't you stay out here with the girly girls, since you care so much about being one?'

I don't give her time to respond. I walk away.

The hallway is empty. The outside heaters are doing their job. There is a door under the stairs which I presume is a toilet, but it's locked. I can hear someone retching and decide not to wait. There must be another bathroom upstairs.

The landing is as plush as the hallway, circular and lined with professional photographs of Tadhg and his family. His father looks just like him, though less chiselled in the jawline. But there is also an older girl in the photographs. She sits in front of Tadhg with a resigned look on her face. I am trying to guess her age when a door beside me opens.

'Can I help you?'

It's her – the girl from the photograph.

'I was just looking for a bathroom.'

She points back down the stairs. 'There's one in the hallway.'

'Yeah, I know. It's being decorated by an over-enthusiastic drinker.'

'Oh god, not a vomiter! I told Mum and Dad you were too young to be given drink. Where's Tadhg? I bet he doesn't give a damn.'

'He was out in the garden last time I saw him.'

She takes in a deep breath and points to another door off the landing. 'There's a bathroom there. Try not to puke.'

'I'm not drunk. I've only had one drink. I don't really like it.'

'Don't care. Just be quick and then tell Tadhg he had better get the bathroom downstairs cleaned up before Mum and Dad get home.'

She disappears back into what I presume is her bedroom, shutting the door firmly behind her.

The bathroom is nearly as big as my bedroom at home. It has a free-standing bath with beautiful ornate legs and the handbasin is not marble but a polished stone that resembles sandstone. Not that I'm some bathroom nerd, but I do excel in geography.

I'm so preoccupied with the handbasin that I forget to lock the bathroom door. I sit down on the toilet. When the door opens, I nearly dribble the remaining pee over the polished floor.

'Oh for fuck's sake.' It's Tadhg's sister, staring at me from the open doorway. 'Don't you lock doors after you?'

I'm mortified. I just stand there pulling up my jeans as quickly as I can.

She starts laughing. 'You should see your face.'

'I don't need to see it. I can imagine. It feels hot.'

'What's your name?'

'Ros.'

'Well, Ros, why don't you wash your hands. I'll be waiting outside.'

'It's all yours,' I say, wiping my wet hands on the back of my jeans.

'Oh, I don't need the bathroom. I was looking for you.'

'Why?'

She pauses slightly, as if wondering whether looking for me has been a good idea now that she has found me.

'I was a bit rude when we met earlier. I just get frustrated when Mum and Dad expect me to look after everything when they're out. I'm only two years older than Tadhg and he doesn't listen to me. He's a brat. But then, you must know that.'

I don't really know what to say. Am I supposed to diss her brother? I'm at his party. She might tell him if I slag him off for being arrogant and entitled. Anyway, she is just as entitled.

'He's OK.'

She laughs again. 'Well, that's faint praise. I will go and tell him now how much you like him.'

Being teased by her is strangely pleasing.

'Do you smoke?' she continues.

'No. Why?'

'God, you're boring. You don't drink and you don't smoke. What do you do for fun?'

'I pee at parties with the door open.'

It's unlike me, pointing out my failings. But I didn't know what else to say. I don't want her to think I'm boring.

'I'm Eddy,' she says. 'With a "Y". I had to shorten the unbelievable travesty of a moniker my parents gave me – Edwina, after my grandaunt. She left my father the money. The money which became all this.' She points to the chandelier hanging down through the centre of the hallway. 'It also pays for this,' she adds, taking a spliff from her shirt pocket. 'But if you don't smoke there's no point sharing it with you.'

Out of a desire to impress Eddy, I am soon sitting on the floor of her bedroom, puffing the smoke towards the open window above our heads.

'Your first spliff?'

'Not at all,' I lie, trying to contain the desire to cough.

'When was your first, then? You must be – what, just sixteen?'

'I'm seventeen. Last week, twenty-fourth of October.'

'You're old for TY.'

'The oldest in my year.'

'How come?'

'I missed a year, when I was twelve.'

'Tell me more.'

I shake my head and she lets the topic drop. For which I'm grateful.

'Twenty-fourth of October. Did you enjoy your birthday? I will remember for next year and send you a birthday card.' She takes the spliff from my hand and has a long drag. 'A Sagittarius. Loyal and assertive. But usually extroverts.'

'I don't know. I've never looked into my star sign.'

'You see, even that's so Sagittarian. I'm Aquarius, the water carrier. I had my whole chart done once. My mother is really into this stuff. But then she's into lots of whacky things.'

'My mother is into her writers' group, but they don't seem to do much writing. Just a lot of wine drinking and criticising.'

Eddy seems interested in this piece of information. 'Oh, what does she write? I'm studying English. I want to be a journalist. Or a fiction writer. Of course, neither makes any money unless you're a celebrity to start off with. Not that that matters in my case, thanks to my namesake.'

I take the spliff back from her. I'm enjoying the mellow feeling it's giving me. I don't feel anxious about anything, for a change. Maybe this is the answer to dukkha.

'I don't know what Mum writes. She just sits at the kitchen table and throws a lot of scrunched-up paper in the bin.'

Eddy undoes the buttons of her sleeves and pushes them up to her elbows. 'I always get hot when I smoke. Do you find that?'

She knows I don't smoke, but I say, 'Sometimes.'

'If I was on my own, I'd take off all my clothes and just sit here naked. With the room locked of course, not like you.'

She stands up from the floor and I pray that she won't start undressing. I know spliffs do strange things to people, even if I haven't had one before. However, she is heading towards a speaker, her phone in her hand.

'Do you like Morrison?'

I look at her blankly.

'Van the Man!' she says with some exasperation. 'You must have heard of him. I don't really like much of today's stuff. Its's too anodyne. I prefer the oldies. Obviously there's some new stuff I like, do you like Mitski?'

'I like Nirvana.' Not exactly the newest, I know. And I don't like it anyway. It's too aggressively noisy for me. But it sounds cooler than admitting to Billie Eilish and I don't have a clue who Mitski is. I don't listen to music.

She turns to face me. 'Nirvana's just too loud, too in-your-face for me. I get the sentiment. I just don't like the anger behind it. Do you know what I mean? I like ballads like this one. It's my favourite. It's called "Sweet Thing". Van's lyrics are poetry to music. Have you heard this before?'

But I don't need to answer her. She has moved on. She is singing another song that I have never heard before. She has a nice voice, soft and melodic.

'What's that you're singing?'

'I don't know exactly. It's lyrics born out of a haze of weed. I love making up lyrics. It's my two favourite things combined – poetry and music. One day I will write a song just for you.'

For the second time in her company, I blush.

1.30am
Friday
27 Beechfield Drive

It is way past midnight. I can't remember how I got home. It's a blur, really. I was sitting there listening to Van the Man and then I was here, explaining to my mother how the film night ran late as there was a sequel. She looked at me strangely and then must have decided she was too tired for a conversation. I could be dealt with in the morning.

In bed I search Spotify for the Van Morrison track, hoping I can recognise Eddy's favourite music again. Another night, I would just give up and go to sleep, but this is not just any night.

When I find the song, I feel I am back in her bedroom again, watching her singing, swaying to the music, asking me to dance with her. Of course, I'd refused at first. I don't dance. Beasts don't dance. But she had reached out to me and pulled me up from the floor.

'Yes you do, everybody dances.'

Without the weed, I wouldn't have danced. I would have left.

I put my phone down on the bed and pick up my journal. It seems only right to commit the evening to crisp white pages. But I don't know what to write. For the first time, I am lost for words. They usually flow, but now they're abandoning me. I can't leave the page empty with just a title. So I write the lyrics of her song, the one born from smoking dope.

> *The first time I met you I knew you were the one,*
> *I held you in my arms and my life truly begun,*
> *We laughed and we danced, and sang listening to rain,*
> *And I never want to be without you again.*
> *Dance with me, dance with me,*
> *Let me be the one.*
> *Dance with me, dance with me,*
> *Until the day is done.*

Maybe that's the way to avoid feeling empty. Maybe to avoid pain would be to dance with Eddy for ever.

11.20am
Friday
School concourse

'Hey, Ros, what the hell happened to you last night?' It is one of the Flock. Rachel Maguire. Not someone who usually gives me the time of day. 'Come here.'

Reluctantly I walk over.

'Sarah's pissed off with you. Said you disappeared on her, and she couldn't find you anywhere.'

'Well, that's between me and her.'

Rachel looks at her surrounding entourage of girls to make sure they are being attentive and then she goes in for the kill.

'Well maybe she's jealous.'

'What the hell are you talking about?'

'Tadhg said he saw you in his sister's bedroom last night after everyone else had gone home.'

'Oh, get lost. We were listening to music.'

'Tadhg says she's a dyke, has a girlfriend and every-thing. So I suppose you fitted right in.'

'I'm sure he didn't call his own sister a "dyke".'

They are sniggering now, as the Flock are prone to do. They are looking at me as if I am pathetically out of my depth.

'We always thought you weren't one of us, Ros. Just too... How would you say? Queer. And always looking at Sarah as if you want to jump her. I suppose she's furious with you for making out with Tadhg's sister.'

I don't answer. I turn and walk away. But I can feel them all watching me.

I have never skipped class before. Many do, but they are usually rounded up from the various bathrooms by patrolling teachers. I decide the prop room at the back of the auditorium is the best place to hide. It's small, dark and full of hats, fake beards and other weird items from various school plays. I sit on a large amplifier and try on one of the musty beards. There is a cracked mirror hanging on the back of the door. The beard strangely suits me. I don't look like a girl pretending to be a man. I just look older. Like my father. The same piercing blue eyes and thin mouth. I am a prime candidate for fillers. I know some of the Flock have already investigated how much it costs. The Flock. I hate them so much.

I know I'm not a 'dyke', as they call it. Sometimes I wish I was. It would be simpler. And at least I would have my tribe. People to have my back.

I take the beard off and throw it back into the box. It doesn't surprise me that Eddy has a girlfriend. She is beautiful. Beautiful people are never on their own for long. They always find someone to love them. And she seems so mature, though she's only two years older than me. Maybe less.

'What do you want to do when you go to college?' she had asked.

'I don't know,' I had replied. 'Maybe engineering. My dad's an engineer and I think his job is interesting. He's not stuck in an office all day. I don't think I'd like a job where I'm always in one place.'

She had nodded as if she had found what I said interesting, but I knew she was pretending. I am boring. And last night I didn't want her to think I was boring.

The only topic I really know about is sports. I don't know how to be bohemian and interesting, even when slightly high. Smoking the spliff is the most radical thing I have ever done.

And now I am doing the second most radical thing. I'm mitching. At least I have chosen a warm place to hide. There is a set of industrial-looking pipes running around the floor of the room. Sitting with my back against the wall, I warm up nicely. It takes me a few minutes to realise that I'm crying. I thought the embarrassing tears had stopped as I fled the concourse, but they are still rolling softly on to the collar of my shirt. I hate being called gay. It's just the injustice of it all. Nothing against gays, but *I'm* not gay. That's the one thing I'm sure of. I want to be with women, just not in this bloody body. How messed-up is that?

I want to be in a male body, with a girlfriend who sees my masculinity. I want to be a husband and have a wife. But I know it can't happen unless I come out of my shell and tell someone. Unless I am brave enough to have surgery and kill off Rosalyn Hughes.

I hate being Rosalyn. So why am I so loath to end her life?

I do this. I talk about my life in the third person. It gives me the distance that I prefer. Rosalyn Hughes is like a character in a soap opera to me. She is as unreal as any TV character. I never acknowledge her existence in real life. That is because there is no female version of me inside my head.

Whoever anyone else thinks they are talking to doesn't exist. And that's because I'm male. But you don't see it. It's buried underneath this embarrassing exterior. Sometimes I stand in front of my bedroom mirror, and I look at my face and I can't see Rosalyn Hughes, the schoolgirl. I just see the real me. But the male looking back at me in the mirror can only exist if I am brave enough to step out from the shadows.

I have read about it – so-called 'transformational' surgery, hormone therapy, counselling – but I can't walk up to my parents and look them in the face and tell them I'm not their daughter, and I never have been. My mum would go into freefall. She has a future planned for me where she is the mother of the bride, buying the hat and sitting proudly at the top table, while my father raises a glass in toasting.

Speaking of which, I'm over-toasting. I need to move away from the pipes behind my back or I will melt.

When the door to the prop room opens, I feel more naked than on the toilet in Tadhg's house.

Mr Cunningham stands in front of me looking less than impressed.

'Rosalyn Hughes, what are you doing in here? There are people searching the school for you. You know you can't miss roll time without an excuse.'

He looks at me as if he is going to rain hell and then he notices my tears.

'Are you OK? This is not like you. There are others I'd expect to find mitching, but not you.'

If any teacher is to discover my refuge, I am happy it is Mr Cunningham. He has the insight to notice if something is not quite right. He also has a bit more humanity than some of the other teachers. He doesn't seem to see us all as public enemy number one.

'Your friends are worried about you. They said you were unwell after drinking at a party last night. If that's true, then you should be with the nurse, not hiding out in a storeroom.'

I wipe my tears away with a shirt sleeve and give Mr Cunningham an accusatory look.

'Which friends?'

'I don't want to drop them in it. They were only concerned for your well-being.'

'I don't care, sir. Which friends?'

'Rachel and Jackie.'

The bloody Flock! Typical.

'They're not my friends, sir.'

Mr Cunningham shrugs his shoulders. 'Well, I hope you weren't drinking last night. You're still too young, you know.'

'I know, sir. And I don't drink.'

'So why are you mitching class, then? Anything else going on?'

Anything else going on? I repeat the question in my head. I'm a walking time-bomb of things that could go wrong and suddenly blow up in my face. And I can list them all.

I have parents who are only interested in their perfect son.

A wonderful friend, who is angry with me.

A college student who has broken down my defences.

And now some of the bitchy girls in my class think I'm gay.

Will I explain all that to you, Mr Cunningham, or will I let you think I'm suffering from a hangover? Or I could tell you the ultimate secret.

You, Mr Cunningham, are talking to a male. And I hate the fact that all you see is a female.

But if I explain the truth to you, you'll send me to Dolly, aka Ms McGlynn, the disaster of a counsellor who everyone avoids like the plague. She has a fake smile and a barrage of cringy self-help books that are frightening.

'I should go back to class, sir.'

'Not that simple, I'm afraid. You're going to have to be written up for detention.'

'But, sir, I've never done this before. I was just upset about something.'

'I'm sorry, Ros, but Ms Harrison is not going to accept an apology. She's on the warpath and detention is the punishment for mitching class. You know all this.'

I nod my head. I'm not worried about sitting in detention next Wednesday. I've no hockey match next week. It's just telling my parents. They would have to sign the detention slip. I would never hear the end of it. And then there's Ian. He has gone through the whole of school without a single detention. He's just so bloody irritating.

'Go back to class, Rosalyn, and you'll be hearing from Ms Harrison, I'm sure. But whatever is bothering you, talk to someone rather than hiding away. OK?'

I nod my head and leave to go back to class.

It takes me ages to find them. There has been a change to the timetable. Three teachers are out sick, so TY have been sent to the lecture hall for a video on the latest devastation to the planet. Orangutans standing on chopped trees, baring their teeth in anger. It's going down well with the year. It has the feeling of *Planet of the Apes* meets *Avatar*. Mankind is the greedy enemy.

I scan the hall, looking for a friendly face. Luckily, Sarah is sitting on one of the lower rows with a spare seat beside her.

'Ros, what's got into you?'

'I feel sick, Sarah. Probably the drink last night. I told you I'm not used to it.'

'You're lucky the bell had gone before you came back. Harrison was furious. She sent Rachel and Jackie to find you.'

'I know. They told Cunningham I had been drinking last night and was ill.'

'God, the dirty snitches. What did he say?'

'I told him it was a lie, and I was just upset about something. You know Cunningham, he's a softy. He just let me go with a detention. To be honest, I was so relieved that he didn't send me to Viper.'

We all hate Viper. The assistant principal in charge of discipline. He has a quick temper and piercing black eyes. His real name is Doherty, but none of the students call him that. Even some of the younger teachers have been overheard using the nickname.

'So where did you go last night? I looked everywhere for you. I thought we were going home together. You know I hate walking home alone in the dark.'

'I'm sorry. I just had too much to drink. I fell asleep in an upstairs bedroom. When I woke up you were gone.'

Sarah doesn't look convinced. 'It's not what everyone else is saying, Ros.'

'Well, if you're going to listen to anything the Flock say, you're hardly listening to the truth.'

I expect her to reply, but she looks away and starts up a conversation with Ray. He is one of the few boys who will sit next to girls in class. He doesn't really mind the teasing. He fancies Sarah and everyone knows it, including Sarah.

4.30pm
Friday
27 Beechfield Drive

It's so good to be home in my own space again. Not only do I shut my bedroom door, but I lock it. I don't want to be disturbed. I flop down on my bed and take my phone out of my pocket. There are no messages. I half expect one from Sarah. We usually text after school every day. We talk about everything that has happened in the classes we don't have together.

I put in my headphones and play my favourite new song, 'Sweet Thing'.

Last night I had aged listening to that song. I was transported into an older version of me. A version that was more mature and worldly. I had smoked a spliff and discussed the beauty of Thomas Hardy's work. Not that I had ever read any of his books. It hadn't been necessary. Eddy had read them all. She just needed me to agree with her understanding of his writing.

'He challenged the attitudes to sexuality, religion and class at the time,' she said, her hand making a swirl of smoke in the air with the joint. 'Do you know that publishers rejected his first novel, and he burned the manuscript? I love that about him, such passion that he couldn't bear his words to fail. What are you passionate about, Ros?'

I didn't answer her question. I didn't get the chance to. I had never been kissed by a girl before. It was everything that I had dreamt of. It was soft and gentle, or do those words hold the same meaning? I'm really no good at English, even though I love words.

The thought of her kissing me brings tears to my eyes because I have opened a Pandora's box of complexities. She is gay. I am not. I am someone who loves my own sex from a different perspective. I just need the words to explain it to the world. Maybe I can explain it to Eddy if I ever see her again. I can't even remember if we exchanged numbers. I can only remember the song, the singing, the kiss, and a whole pile of useless facts about Thomas Hardy. Although I do remember that he was someone who challenged attitudes to sexuality. I wish our world did more of that. I know it's better now than it used to be, but if the Flock still give me a hard time for being gay, what would they do if they knew I was transgender?

Last night was cosmic in my life. The real me had come alive. I had been alive with her.

I want to write it all down and commit the experience to more than just my memory. I'm afraid I will forget the evening, and that it will fade into just another dream. Yet when I write the words in my journal, I feel the maturity slipping away from me, and I feel like a child struggling to survive in an older world. She's in university. She's learning English, sitting in lecture halls with other intellectual students discussing authors and using poetic language. We have nothing in common. Nothing to keep the moment extended. I'm a TY student, just out of braces and still trying to pick subjects for my Leaving Certificate.

Our world does not intersect except for one area, the existence of her irritating brother. I can hardly ask him for her phone number or turn up at his front door without the rest of my year knowing.

I shut my eyes and try to imagine her lying beside me on the bed. Maybe my imagination is the only place we will ever meet again.

> Hello, sweet thing.

I don't recognise the number. I think I know who the text is from, but I'm scared to believe it.

> Hi, who's this?

> Funny, sweet thing, it's Eddy.

I just look at the screen. No matter how many times I read the words, they mean the same thing. It's her.

> Do you think I'm a baby-snatcher, Ros?

I can't think anything bad about her. I think she is funny and interesting and very beautiful. My phone lights up again.

> Ouch. The lack of reply is ominous. I'm not 19 until Feb, it's less than two years, the gap between us.

Quickly I write a reply.

> I don't think you're a baby snatcher. Because I'm not a baby.

> I agree. You seem so much more mature than Tadhg. Who is a bit of an arse anyway.

I laugh. She's right about her brother. He's immature in the worst sense of the word. My fingers quickly type another reply. I don't want the texting to end.

> I've been listening to Van the Man today.

> ☺

> But the song I liked most last night was yours, Eddy.

Really?!?!

I continue with some of her lyrics.

Dance with me, dance with me. Let me be the one. Dance with me, dance with me. Until the day is done.

Another smiling emoji comes back with a ping and then a short message.

I loved dancing with you last night, Ros.

Me too, Eddy, its why I love your song.

That's so cute of you.

☺

The messages stop then. For one horrible minute my phone is silent. Maybe that's it, a brief exchange of messages and she will go back to her college world. Back to her girlfriend.

Are you still there, Ros? Sorry my mum came in. Was complaining of the stink in the downstairs toilet. I told her she shouldn't have let Tadhg's party have alcohol. She just laughed and told me I was a party pooper. Parents! So bloody frustrating.

Mine are worse. They wouldn't even let me have a party.

Got to go, Ros, have an essay to write for tomorrow. Glad you're chilled about last night as I didn't want to leave anything funny between us.

No problem, Eddy. Take care.

What the hell! Who writes *Take care* at the end of messages? What am I? Forty years of age? Talk about blowing it! I could have written *See you soon* or something, which leaves things open for another meeting. *Take care* sounds like I'm not interested. Maybe she found my writing her lyrics in a message too cheesy? Maybe I appeared too eager.

I re-read all the messages and then re-read them again. Then once more just to see if I can pick up any nuances from the words. Is she just thanking me for a lovely evening and making sure I'm not throwing up somewhere from smoking weed?

Oh god I hope not. I hope she is thinking of me the way I'm thinking of her.

When my mum knocks on my bedroom door, I almost hit the ceiling with anxiety. I hide my phone under my pillow as if she is going to interrogate me about messages that she doesn't even know exist.

'Rosalyn, why do you lock your bedroom door? It's not necessary, you know. Everyone respects everyone else's privacy in this house.'

I look at her and just feel the frown spreading across my face.

She ignores my angst.

'What did you want me to sign after dinner? You said something about a form? Are you going on another TY trip? I'm sorry I forgot to answer you. It's just your brother was explaining his plans for the summer. Backpacking with Johnno to Thailand and Vietnam. Isn't that great? He will have such an adventure. Wish I was twenty years younger, I'd go with him myself.'

'That would be creepy, Mum. Don't say those things out loud please.'

'Don't be so critical, Rosalyn, you know what I mean.'

It is probably not the best idea, irritating my mother before I ask her to sign my detention slip.

'Sorry. I'm just in a bit of a mood. I've had a horrible day. In fact, I was given detention.'

I expect an angry reaction, but she just looks at me slightly perplexed.

'That's not like you, Ros. Everything OK? What did you do to get detention?'

I'm tempted to say that I just forgot my homework but that would never warrant a detention and I don't want her to ring Ms Harrison and give out about the unfairness of the punishment.

'I mitched class.'

'What for, in heaven's name?'

Now I must lie. I can't tell her that I was running away from the Flock because they had called me a dyke.

'I had a row with Sarah over something that happened at the party, and I was upset.'

My mother sits on my bed and puts her hand on my arm. 'Oh Rosalyn, do you want me to ring her mum and sort things out between you. Beth and I have always been able to get you two back together. I'm sure you're only best friends because of us.'

'Jesus, no, Mum, I'm not four. I don't need you to interfere in my friendships. I'm just letting you know why I got detention. I mitched class.'

'Everything OK between you and Sarah now?'

'Just sign the form please, Mum. I can't hand it back without a signature from a parent. Don't make me wish I'd forged it.'

'Goodness, Rosalyn, you can be so tetchy. I hope it's just a phase, from all those raging hormones. Mind you, Ian never went through that. He seemed to have no problem.'

I'm relieved when she leaves the room. Not that I don't love my mum. It's just that we have a mile of ground between us. She is from one planet, and I am definitely from another. Like that book my dad gave her ages ago – *Men are from Mars, Women are from Venus*. I hate the title of that book. So insulting to everyone else that exists out there. It's just a mash of silly stereotypes that makes life more difficult for people like me. Not all men and women behave the same. I'm from bloody Pluto, so where's that in your binary book?

I can hear my phone letting out a muffled ping. If it is Eddy, I'm going to be so happy.

It's school. My match has been changed from Saturday to Wednesday and now I'm going to miss it, sitting in detention. Coach will be furious, and he will also be having one of those awkward conversations with Mr Whelan over why rugby players can miss detention, but hockey players can't.

But it's not the thought of missing my match that keeps me from sleeping.

Will I ever see Eddy again?

2pm
Wednesday
Detention hall

I haven't talked to Sarah for a week. She seems angry with me, and I'm unsure about how to approach it. I don't really want to ask her what's wrong. I don't want to address the rumours that are still circulating from the party. I just want to keep my head down until things go back to normal between us. They always do. We have known each other too long.

I have never been in detention before. It's so boring – an hour of sitting and writing out answers to questions that are totally meaningless. The only, unwanted relief from the boredom is Tadhg. He is sitting in the row behind me. His rugby match has been cancelled, so he has been sent to complete one of his many detentions. I try to ignore him from the minute he enters the room. I pretend to be engrossed in the random task we have been assigned. I'm making a mockery of the answers. There is no way old Badger is going to read our detention work. He never even corrects homework. So I invent my answers, knowing I'm safe in my little rebellion.

A note lands on my desk, I nearly miss it as it bounces towards the edge of the table. I open it reluctantly.

DIKE

Idiot. He can't even spell it.

I scrunch the note up and throw it towards the bin in the corner. My aim is unerringly accurate, and it sails in.

When the next note lands in front of me, I turn around and glare at Tadhg without opening it. He doesn't flinch but raises an eyebrow and grins at me like some demented loon. The third note hits me on the back of the head. He doesn't like being ignored so he starts coughing out the word *dyke* as if no one will notice his attempts at bullying.

Badger looks up from *The Irish Times* and scans the room. He waggles a fat finger, at no one in particular, and turns his gaze back to the paper.

Another piece of scrunched-up paper hits me on the back of the head.

I want to turn around and shout at Tadhg. Tell him to go and die. But I don't want to give him the satisfaction of knowing that I'm irritated by his behaviour. I'm trying to be rational in response to this moron. Hopefully, he will give up when he gets bored with my lack of reaction. Sometimes, though, even when you think you are in control of your emotions, they burst out at the most unhelpful moments.

This is one of those moments. I don't see it coming. I just erupt uncontrollably. Years of trying to suppress how I feel escape in a torrent of anger.

I turn around and throw my pen at him.

He looks stunned at first, and then lets out a yelp of pain. It's because my aim has been too successful. The point of the pen is embedded in the corner of his eye and a small trickle of blood makes its way down his cheek.

Time freezes then. The whole detention hall is captured in one horrifying moment, and the onlookers are pulling faces of horror. Badger jumps up from behind his desk, dropping his newspaper to the floor. Tadhg sits there with his mouth open, the pen hanging hideously. He seems afraid to touch it in case it removes his eyeball. Most of the other students are now up from their desks and circling around him, taking pictures with their phones.

'Put your phones away,' Badger shouts, waving them back to their seats. 'They're supposed to be in your lockers.'

Tadhg has found his voice. 'That bitch threw her pen at me, sir.'

Badger looks at me with a mixture of horror and confusion.

'Don't use that language in here, Morrisey,' he says, trying to take control of the situation, although you can see he is unsure of what school procedure to follow next. 'Cole, go to the front office and get the nurse and the assistant principal.'

This is the end of me. I am going to be suspended. Or worse – expelled.

There is zero tolerance for physical violence in our school. Viper has always been very strict on discipline. And now I might have blinded another student. And not just any student, but the captain of the beloved rugby team. And what excuse can I give for my behaviour? I don't want to tell anybody that Tadhg has called me a dyke. I don't want them all looking at me and sizing up my behaviour to see if there's any truth in it. And I don't want my parents even considering it.

The nurse walks in, followed by Viper. Nothing is said by either of them. The nurse calmly removes the pen from the corner of Tadhg's eye and takes him out of the room. Viper points towards the open doorway for me to leave with him. He says nothing until we reach his office.

'Sit out in the corridor and wait for me to make a few phone calls.'

I nod. What else can I do? Although I'm thinking of making a break for it. My grandparents live in Sandycove, and they are away at the moment. I could get the DART down the coast and just hide out in their house. I have a spare key. I even know their alarm code. It would be better than facing the music. Looking into the disappointed faces of my parents, and knowing they are wondering where they went wrong after the paragon of virtue that is Ian. I'm also terrified of Viper. The thought of being in his office gives me nausea.

And then there's Tadhg. What will his parents say? Will he be blind in one eye from my moment of stupidity? And Eddy? Jesus, what will she think? My mind is racing through countless outcomes.

I decide to make a run for it. To go to Sandycove. But it is too late. The door opens and Viper beckons me into his lair.

He holds out a chair. He is being almost nice, which is even more disconcerting.

'Rosalyn, would you like to explain what has just happened in the detention hall?'

It is difficult to know what to say, so I lie. I know how to lie. I have done it all my life. I have pretended to be someone I'm not. I have pretended to like things I hate. And I have bought into a future that I know doesn't belong to me.

I am even dressed in a lie. I walk into school in a skirt rather than trousers. I don't want anyone questioning my sexual preferences or gender. Only the 'odd' girls wear trousers. The rest of us freeze in winter for the prize of fitting into the acceptable norm. Trouser-wearing is seen as the dress of the lesbian girls or the alternative thinkers. Skirt-wearing admits you to the feminine tribe. It is taking your place amongst the accepted. Hiding myself means wearing a skirt every day, even though I belong in a pair of trousers.

'Tadhg's pen ran out, so he threw a note at me asking for a lend of one. I turned and threw a pen at him. It wasn't meant to hit him in the eye. It was an accident.'

Viper says nothing but twirls a pen between his long thin fingers.

'Is he going to be OK?' I continue, trying to seem considerate and contrite.

'He is in A&E having it checked,' Viper responds. 'His mother is with him and she's not best pleased, as you can imagine, Rosalyn.'

'I'm sorry, sir.'

He shrugs his shoulders and scrawls a few words on a piece of paper. 'Sorry is an easy word to say, Miss Hughes, but it doesn't solve anything. Your mother should be here in a few minutes. It might be best if you go home for the rest of the day until the school finds the truth behind this incident. You say it's an accidental injury. Tadhg might see it differently.'

Of course Tadhg will see it differently. He will bury me with a different version of events. But he will omit the bullying notes. He can't be tarnished with those. Every wellbeing class we have had since first year has warned us against bullying behaviour, and especially homophobia.

My mother is at the door. I can see her face through the small rectangular window. She looks upset.

'Mrs Hughes, nice to see you again.'

My mother gives a weak smile and holds out a hand to Viper. I wouldn't want to shake the man's hand. It is spider like, long fingered with chunky knuckles, and I imagine his palms being constantly sweaty.

'We have never had you in the office before for a difficult conversation. To be quite frank, I'm surprised at what's happened. Rosalyn says it was an accident. But throwing a pen into someone's eye is reckless, even if it is an accident. We can't have missiles in the classroom.'

My mother looks at me and takes a deep breath.

'I hope you've apologised, Rosalyn, for your reckless behaviour. Mr Doherty is right. You can't be throwing things around a classroom.'

I nod my head. I'm not too sure I want to say anything. I might incriminate myself. My lie is probably going to backfire on me anyway.

'I think you should take Rosalyn home, Mrs Hughes, and when we find out how Tadhg is and learn his version of events, we can make a decision about what form of punishment this incident requires. As you know, we have zero tolerance for violence, so let's hope that this is just an unfortunate accident. I will ring you tomorrow and we can take it from there.'

My mother doesn't reply. She just decides to go for a closing handshake and ushers me out of the room.

4pm
Wednesday
27 Beechfield Drive

I look down at my journal, but again I don't know what to write. I draw instead. Big bold lettering making angry words on the page. The words are surrounded by bolts of lightning, and pens which look like missiles. Our year one English teacher once told us that the pen is mightier than the sword, and I have just used a blue biro as a weapon against my bully. I can still see it hanging out of the corner of his eye and the little trickle of blood on his cheek.

I must be devoid of feelings, as I don't feel sorry for him at all. I'm almost glad I did it. I don't have remorse. But I should. What type of person injures another without any care for their health?

But then I still eat meat too. And last week a person from some animal rescue group gave us a lecture on animal welfare. Half of the girls gave up meat that day and became vegetarians. They cried copious tears over all the little pigs that had died to provide them with sausages. Some even went vegan. But I didn't. Maybe I'm slightly psychotic. Or is that the right illness for someone who doesn't have empathy for other beings?

I look down at my journal. I am no longer drawing pens. A repeated word has appeared. Randomly covering every inch of the page. I have drawn the 'E' like two semi circles one on top of the other and the bottom of the 'd's have formed a pair of eyes. Underscoring the whole word is the tail of a flamboyant 'y'.

What will she think of me when she finds out I have attacked her brother with a pen?

My phone pings. It's going to be her. Our connection is already so strong that she knows I'm thinking about her. I have summoned her through writing her name in my journal.

But it's my brother. And Ian never texts me.

> Are you OK

Not only does he never text me, but he never asks how I am. So this is a worrying interest in my welfare.

> I'm fine. Why?

> Mum texted me

> Thinks you will be suspended

> What the hell! Why would she text you?

Dunno. She asked me did I
know Tadhg's family. I told
her his sister was in my
class. She asked me were
they reasonable people!
Why did you throw a pen
at him?

He knew Eddy! I had never thought about it before. Of
course he did. They were the same age. But maybe she was
just in his year. Maybe he didn't know her well.

Was his sister in your
actual class?

Yes

Shit, he did know her well.

Why did you throw a pen at
him? You told mum it was
an accident. I'm guessing it
wasn't

IT WAS AN ACCIDENT!!!

Really??? Your temper and your aim! I doubt it was an accident

I ask Ian the question that is niggling me.

So how well do you know his sister? Is she a friend of yours? What's she like? He's a moron

Frustratingly my brother misses his cue.

So why did you launch a pen at him

I'm not telling you.

Jesus Ros you'd better hope his eye is OK. You could be expelled for this

I know

Look don't worry just stick to your story and keep saying you're sorry

But Tadhg didn't ask me for a pen. He'll drop me in it for sure.

> Have to go. I've got training.
> But just chill.
> It'll be fine.

Easy for him to say. I'm so close to having my life ruined. I don't like school, except for hockey, but I don't want to be expelled. I'm not like Paddy Fitzpatrick. I'm not a rebel. I don't want to be the centre of attention.

Another ping on my phone. I don't need any more 'brotherly advice' from Ian.

> Hi Ros

It's her. She must know what I've done to her brother. What do I say? I can't take long thinking. She will know I have read her message. She will have seen the two little blue ticks. I panic.

> I'm sorry about Tadhg.
> Is he OK?

> Tadhg?!? Why??

Oh god, she doesn't know. What do I write now?

> I threw a pen at him.
> It hit his eye.
> I thought you'd know.

The reply is not what I expect. Just three laughing emojis. She thinks it's funny! And then:

> I do know. Mum took him to A&E. His eye is fine.

> Are your parents angry with me?

> God no! Accidents happen. Just unfortunate.

Accidents happen? Did Tadhg not say I attacked him? Why wouldn't he have told them the truth?

> What are you doing this weekend?

Why is she asking me? I'm doing what I usually do – playing hockey and sitting in my bedroom listening to Billie Eilish. I decide to play it cool.

> Nothing much

> Good. You can come to a party with me.

I feel suddenly sick. A wave of nausea moves right through me. I can't meet her again. Every inch of me would love to, but I can't step out of my constructed reality. I have a safe world. I have a life that centres around a lie. How can I shatter that lie? Rosalyn Hughes will cease to exist. And although I hate her, I don't know how to be the real me. I've had no practice.

Eddy is real. She's out there. Not hidden from life. She knows who she is, and she lives it. But I'm a captive of my fear. I can't be open about who I am.

I've taken too long to reply to her text.

> Ros, don't you want to party with me again?

I read the words over and my fingers hit the answer before my brain can respond.

> Yes

> Great. It's at a friend's house. Saturday night. We can meet outside Murphy's at 9.

Cool. See you there.

I feel sick again. What the hell am I thinking? How can I go to a party? How can I meet her outside a pub at nine? I'm in TY not first year college. And Mum's still furious with me for attacking Tadhg, so there is no way I will be let out to go to a party. I'm going to be grounded for at least a month.

'Ros, could you come down here please? I've just had Mr Doherty on the phone.'

Brilliant. Viper has called. My fate has been decided already.

My mother is chopping onions with a tear in her eye. I hope the tears are from the onions and not from her phone call with Viper.

'He's such a nice man, Rosalyn, Mr Doherty. He is very understanding.'

'I don't like him.'

'Well, I think you're lucky, Rosalyn, that he's so reasonable. Seemingly Tadhg Morrisey is going to be fine. He's had his eye examined and there's no lasting damage, thank God. The school is still unhappy that you threw the pen towards him, but they are willing to note it as an unfortunate accident.'

I nod at my mum, but I'm shocked. Why had Tadhg corroborated my version of events?

'You're very lucky, Rosalyn, that it's all worked out this way. You're to promise me that you won't throw any pens ever again?'

'I'm not three, Mum.'

'Well stop acting like you are, then.'

The onion, more finely chopped than usual, is thrown into a frying pan.

'As soon as I have this lasagne in the oven, we are driving over to the Morriseys for you to apologise in person.'

'No way. I'm not apologising to him.'

'Rosalyn, this is not a request. It's what's happening. I've already talked to his mother. She seems a lovely woman. She was very sympathetic. Good god, she would have every right to be less understanding.'

5.30pm
Wednesday
The Lodge

I don't know what to say or how I will look Tadhg in the face. My mother is sitting in the living room with the plush Persian carpets and leather sofas, politely exchanging views on how we've all survived a pandemic only to be thrust into a world of war and refugees. They seem to have decided that the pen-throwing will not be their main topic of conversation. It was only an accident, no damage done.

I have been left sitting in the kitchen at the large marble island, waiting for Tadhg to come down from his bedroom. His mother has decided that giving us space to talk will be less cringy for us. She is so unlike my mum. She doesn't micromanage her children's lives. But then, Eddy thinks her parenting skills are poor and that her brother needs a few more shackles.

'This is awkward for you.' Tadhg is standing in the doorway, smirking at me. There is a patch over his eye.

'Is it sore?'

He shrugs his shoulders. 'Not really.' He walks over to the fridge and opens the door. 'Want a Coke?'

'Yeah, sure.'

He places a cold can in front of me and sits down on a stool.

'You're a fucking lunatic you know. You could have taken my eye out.'

Although his words are confrontational, his tone is decidedly friendly. He seems almost admiring of my aggressive behaviour, as if I've earned his respect.

'You asked for it, Tadhg.'

'Well, the truth obviously hurt you.'

I decide to ignore the jibe. 'Why didn't you tell Viper?'

He takes a drink from the can and pauses over what to say. 'My parents would have gone ape.'

'Why? It was me injured you!'

'Because I called you a dyke! Deborah and Tom hate that sort of thing.'

Deborah and Tom. It sounds weird that he uses their first names so freely, almost as if they aren't his parents at all. I wouldn't want my parents being that laidback with me.

'They've always supported my sister's coming out. They'd go ballistic if they knew.'

'Thing is, I'm not a "dyke", as you call it.'

'What were you doing in my sister's room then?'

'Just chatting.'

'Yeah, right! Chatting about what? She only talks about bloody poetry and that kind of crap.'

I don't get to answer. Eddy is standing in the doorway, hands on her hips, looking angry.

'Jesus, Tadhg, is that why Ros threw a pen at you? You called her a dyke? You're such a neanderthal. Is that what you call me behind my back, you homophobe?'

Tadhg looks genuinely upset. His bravado has disappeared.

'It was just slagging. I didn't mean anything bad by it. You know I'm cool with you.'

Eddy gives him a sharp look. 'You mean you don't want me to tell Deborah or Tom about this?'

'Jesus, Eddy, it was just a slagging that's all. What's there to tell?'

'Well, why don't you fuck off up to your bedroom and I will think about whether I'll tell them about your bullying behaviour.'

Tadhg leaves the kitchen, pushing into Eddy's shoulder as he walks past her.

'I'm sorry about him.'

'There's no need to apologise, Eddy. I should be apologising.'

She sits down beside me and touches my arm lightly with her hand. 'Not at all. He deserved it. But does everyone in school know you're gay? I didn't think you were out.'

I can't tell her that I'm not gay. I don't know how to explain who I am. It sounds weird in my head. It has always sounded weird. It is better for her to believe the more obvious lie.

'I haven't come out at all.'

She looks disappointed. 'Oh, I just thought if he was slagging you about it, people must know.'

'He saw me in your bedroom the night of the party. He told others in our class. He told them you have a long-time girlfriend.'

'Oh, did he now? The little brat.'

She pushes a lock of hair from over her eyes and stares at me intently.

'I'm sorry, Ros. It seems like it's my fault that you've been outed. Are you upset?'

'I don't want to have that label in school. I'm not ashamed of who I am. It's just not me. I've never felt gay.'

She seems to consider my last statement but then ignores it.

'I knew when I was twelve. But Thomas Hardy says it's difficult for women to define their feelings in a language made by men to express theirs.'

'And there's me thinking you only talked that way last night because you were high on weed.'

She laughs and we both smile. It feels good to see her smile, to have been the cause of it.

'It doesn't matter whether you're gay or not anyway. Our sexual preference should be able to change. We shouldn't have to be gay for life. Although I can't see me being any other way. I am confident in who I am. In fact, I'm proud I can stand up and say I'm gay. Some people can't do that in their country, so I know it's a privilege.'

She picks up Tadhg's empty Coke can and throws it into the bin. 'As long as you're free to be with me, that's all that matters.'

I can feel my face blushing. I know it has turned its usual embarrassing shade of red. 'But you have a girl-friend.'

As soon as I say it, I wish I hadn't. It sounds needy, overwhelmingly childish in the face of her obvious maturity.

'I had a girlfriend, and I will again. It might be you if you stop saying silly things. Do you still want to come to the party on Saturday?'

Is she asking because she regrets inviting me? Face to face with my immaturity she may be reconsidering her invite. Our one and only previous meeting had been in a weed-filled haze of music and dance.

'Yes, I'd like to come.'

'Good, I'd like that too. I can bore you with more Hardy quotes.'

3.30pm
Thursday
Religious Education class

'Do you ever ask yourself "Why am I here?"'

Mr Cunningham glares at Carl Flynn to prevent any smart remark from coming and continues with his opening comments on reincarnation.

'The Hindus and Buddhists believe we have all been here many times. We have had more than just this one life. So I am not just Mr Cunningham the teacher. I may have lived in many other times and places of history.'

A hand goes up from the middle row. 'Can you be a different sex too? Like, were you a woman in some of these past lives?'

Mr Cunningham is happy to have the interaction of a question, even if he is not too sure whether it is a landmine that could explode in his face within seconds.

'It is more than likely that not all of my past lives have been male.'

'That's mad, sir,' Carl Flynn interjects. 'You'd look queer in a dress, sir. A right trannie.'

Mr Cunningham is furious. His eyes flash at Carl, and he pulls a detention slip out of his pocket.

'That's too far, Flynn. You know you can't use such derogatory terms. It's disgraceful and unacceptable.'

Carl moves uncomfortably in his seat. 'I'm sorry, sir. I was only joking. I didn't mean anything by it.'

'It's still detention, Carl. I'm really not impressed.'

The class has stopped the usual murmuring and note-passing. The mood has changed in the room. No-one wishes to be the next person to have the dreaded slip of paper. Mr Cunningham sits down and opens his laptop. Without saying another word, he writes a series of questions which appear on the whiteboard.

'Why don't we all answer some questions if we can't be civil about this topic?' Mr Cunningham suggests.

'Nice one, Carl,' Tadhg hisses under his breath.

'Take out a pen and paper and answer these questions about reincarnation. How does it work as a concept compared to the Christian view of a singular life which goes to heaven with the death of the body?'

A hand reluctantly goes up from the front row. 'Sir, I don't have paper with me. Can I go to my locker?'

'Me too, sir. Can I go as well?'

'What do I always tell you in every class? You must come with paper and pens. Just because you're in TY doesn't mean you don't have to work. Just borrow paper. None of you is leaving the room.'

I look at the questions on the whiteboard. They are difficult to answer. We haven't even been taught the topic, but we are supposed to give our opinion on it.

Do we believe in reincarnation and why?

The idea appeals to me. To have possibly lived a life before as a man, to have experienced everything I can't experience now. It is even more edifying to think that if I die today, I may reincarnate as a male.

'Mr Cunningham, do you reincarnate in the same family?'

'The Hindus believe that is possible, Tadhg.'

'God, I hope not. One life with my sister is enough, sir.'

'I'm sure she feels the same way, Tadhg. However, it is a good question. There is an interesting documentary about a boy who was born with a birthmark on the side of his head. His father was shot in the exact same place in a robbery. The family believes that the boy is the reincarnated father.'

The class are all interested in reincarnation now. Murder has been introduced, which has woken up the boys in the back row. They also see a way of avoiding the rest of the questions.

'Can we watch the documentary, sir?'

'Oh, I don't have a copy of it and I'm sure it won't be online. It's from years ago.'

'But maybe we can look on YouTube, sir?'

Mr Cunningham shakes his head. 'Maybe you can answer the questions first. Has anyone answered the first one?'

There is a distinct lack of enthusiasm to reply.

'Jessica, did you get the first one done?'

Mr Cunningham is not stupid. He knows she has answered it. She is the top student in the class. Her future is already mapped. She is going to Africa in the summer to help build houses for the homeless and then she is putting it on her CV so that she can get into Oxford or Cambridge to do international relations.

'I don't believe in reincarnation, sir,' Jessica replies. 'Firstly, I don't believe in God, whether it is Brahman,

Yahweh or Allah. And secondly, I believe that we are purely a set of atoms that dissipate upon death. God is a creation for the weak in order to make them feel safe about their ultimate fate, the finality of death.'

Mr Cunningham is always equal to the task.

'And you're not scared of dying, Jessica?'

'What's the point, sir? We live, we work, we die. It's life. There's no point being scared. It will happen to us all anyway.'

'But Jessica, what if there is reincarnation? How would that impact on your life?'

'It wouldn't impact at all, sir. Even if I was to come back as a slug in a different life.'

A different voice rises above Jessica's. 'Can we come back as slugs, sir?'

'Yes, Conor, some Hindus believe that their atman can be reborn in animal form.'

'Hey, Carl, you're in trouble then. You'll be a worm in the next life!'

A burst of laughter echoes around the room.

'Joking aside,' Mr Cunningham continues, 'the Hindus and Buddhists believe that the bodies we inhabit in this life are just like the clothes we put on. They are not who we are. They are purely our avatars.'

'What, like those tall blue smurfs in that film, sir?'

Mr Cunningham sees the funny side of the comment. 'The original *Avatar* was a great movie. The best 3D technology at the time. It had quite an impact on people when it was released. Have any of you seen it?'

'Can we watch it in class, sir?'

'Actually, we can. We can watch it the week before the Christmas holidays. It's a worthwhile film. I won't spoil it but there are some powerful concepts in it. Basically, it tells us that we are far more than our outer shell. There is one very powerful line where the female lead tells the male lead "I see you". She means she sees below his outer shell into his very soul.'

Jessica gives a snort of derision.

'That's such romantic rubbish, sir. We have no soul. Science has proven –'

'I don't think you can really quote science against the existence of the soul or God. Many scientists believe in God. And, Jessica, if you believe it's all a matter of faith, isn't it important to learn what other people believe so that we can understand their motivations and attitudes?'

Carl is worried that the conversation is moving away from avatars. He is focused on reminding Mr Cunningham to show us the film. 'Sir, are we all avatars with a soul?'

'The Hindus believe so.'

'Is that why some people have sex changes, sir?'

There is an outbreak of jeering around the class.

Carl shrugs his shoulders. 'Hey, it's a genuine question this time.'

'How can you connect Hindu beliefs to sex changes, Carl?'

'Well, say if someone has been a woman in their last ten lives, sir, and now they're a man, maybe they remember being a woman and want to go back to being one. Maybe that's why some people are trans.'

Mr Cunningham looks truly puzzled by this insight. He is not prepared with an answer. He kicks for touch.

'I see where you're coming from, Carl, and we can discuss it at the beginning of next class. The bell's just about to go, so pack away your things.'

The whole room moves in unison. The bell is superfluous now. We have been given permission to move, so we will have the room empty within seconds. However, the conversation has left me reeling.

Is that the case with me? Have I been a man in so many past lives that I crave to be back in that body?

It is a different way of looking at my existence. Maybe I am not such a mistake of creation, after all. Maybe I am just living an echo of my past lives?

9pm
Saturday
Rathmines

I am so nervous. The room is full of girls, with just a few boys melting into the shadows, having deep conversations with beers in their hands.

Eddy is in the centre of the room, kissing a girl on the cheek and holding her hand. I watch them intently. The other girl is very pretty. I am trying to work out if their hand-holding is friendship or is she Eddy's former girlfriend.

'Ros, come over here. I want you to meet Maisie. She's my oldest friend. Been together since preschool. Unfortunately, she's as straight as they come, cos she's so beautiful – inside and out. Don't you think so?'

I don't know how to respond. Maisie is stunning. She has blond hair, a wide smile and perfectly shaped green eyes. The girl smiles as if she knows I'm stuck for words.

'Oy, Ros, eyes off,' Eddy says. 'Come on, let's get a beer.'

Eddy pulls me away to a table in the corner of the room. It's covered in alcohol. Mostly beers but a few odd bottles of vodka and gin.

'Beer? Or would you like something stronger?'

'I don't really drink much.' I wish I hadn't said it. It sounds boring, or as if I'm out of my depth. 'Actually, I'll have a rum and Coke.'

It's something I've heard my mother order. The request comes out of my mouth before my brain engages in the process.

Eddy laughs. 'I think that's a bit rich for us here.'

'Just a beer then,' I reply, flustered by my inadequacy. The bottle is warm but I'm not about to complain.

'Come and meet more of my friends.'

I don't really want to. I just want to be with her. I'd spent two hours deciding which shirt to wear. I tried on so many that my bedroom looked more like a charity shop than the room of someone with OCD. Eventually I decided the deep blue one looked better with my jeans.

I am standing in front of three more girls. They are intelligent-looking – glasses and tied-back hair. They're the opposite to the Flock in school. They're not homogeneous in appearance. One has a tattoo on her neck, and one has bright pink hair. Eddy has momentarily left me with them after introducing us.

'So what are you studying, Ros?'

'I'm on a gap year.' It just comes out. A big fat lie!

'Cool. But why haven't you gone travelling?'

'Yeah, of course I will. It's just my gran is ill, so I'm looking after her until after Christmas.'

I wince at this lie. One of my grandmothers is dead. And the other one is knocking back sangria in Spain. I hope there is no such thing as heaven, or nirvana. Because I hope that my gran's not watching me from the other side, looking at the mess I'm making of my life. Or, even worse, watching me kissing a college student in her bedroom and smoking weed. The thought makes me shiver.

However, among Eddy's friends, there is a murmur of approval at my selfless act.

'You're lucky she's still in your life, Ros. Both my grandparents were dead before I was a teenager.'

Nervously I look around the room.

Please come back, Eddy. I'm drowning in my deceptions.

'So where will you go after Christmas?'

'Thailand probably. Sorry, do any of you know where the bathroom is?'

Smooth escape, idiot! Of course they do.

I breathe a sigh of relief as I lock the door behind me. I'm still clutching the bottle of beer, so I place it on the edge of the sink. I don't really need to pee, but I sit down and try – after checking that the door is locked.

My mind is racing. I have lied to my parents and gone to a party where I know no-one but Eddy. And I have hidden my age and pretended to be one of them. I feel so out of my depth that I can hardly breathe. I just want to stay in the toilet until the party is over and then sneak home. But that's not possible. I can hear someone already at the door, trying the handle, knocking impatiently.

It's one of the boys. He smiles at me as I open the door.

'Sorry about the knocking. Too much beer. Really need a whizz.'

'No, I'm sorry I kept you waiting. Dodgy tummy.'

I sound so false. He doesn't need an explanation.

I find my way to the kitchen where a handful of people are eating nachos and arguing about Putin. They are debating whether someone should assassinate him for the good of mankind. They don't even look up as I enter the room. However, the boy from the toilet appears and decides to put me on the spot.

'Hi, I'm Dermot, the one from the loo. You must be the famous Ros, Eddy's friend. Do you think they should kill Putin?'

'I think someone should. He's a dictator.'

'Ah, but you wouldn't pull the trigger yourself?'

What a strange question! I live in south County Dublin. How would I get to Moscow to assassinate Putin? 'I would if I could.'

He laughs.

'Lies. If I gave you an opportunity and a gun to kill him, you would not pull the trigger. You would happily let someone else do your dirty work, but you would not want the blood on your own hands, the stain on your own soul.'

'That might not be true. If you handed me a gun now, I might shoot you.'

He is amused by my reply. 'I'm sorry. I study ethics. It's part of my DNA to be an asshole and pose difficult questions. Do you want another beer?'

'Yes, if it's cold. The last one was undrinkable.'

He goes to the fridge and comes back with a cold beer. 'Will that suit you better?'

I nod.

'So what do you study?'

'I'm not studying.'

'Makes sense, you're not very good at debating.'

He seems to like teasing me. Strangely I'm not offended. He's easier to talk to than some of the girls. Or maybe I'm just wary of talking to them, afraid that they will see through my lack of femininity.

'So what do you do, then?'

He is persistent.

'I'm on a gap year. Going to Thailand after Christmas.'

'Wow, amazing. How long will you go for? I have some friends heading over next summer. I could put you in touch. Always good to have a friendly face. Actually, you probably know them. Doesn't everyone know everyone in Dublin?'

I smile and take another mouthful of beer. I'm feeling happier now. Repeating the lies is making them easier. 'I'm not sure I want to know anyone else going. Part of the thrill of travelling is to go somewhere you know no-one. You can be anyone you wish then.'

Dermot takes a long swig of his beer and smiles at me.

'What a wonderful way of seeing travel – as an opportunity to reinvent oneself. So if you could be anyone, who would you be?'

For the first time in my life, I could say it. I could hide it in a drunken philosophical conversation. 'I would be a man.'

'Why an earth would you want to be a man? I believe we have had our day. The age of patriarchal domination is coming to an end. Women will be the main voices of our future.'

'Is that what you really think?'

He nods his head. 'Of course. Look at the changes happening. Women are now being given an equal voice. Yes there are those still fighting against it, hoping to prevent the old order from crumbling, but otherwise the worm has turned.'

His eyes almost sparkle with a passion for his topic.

'So you see, Ros, being a woman today *is* better than being a man. The future is yours.'

'It's not the future we are talking about, Dermot. You asked me who I would like to be now, and I would like to be a man. I mightn't want to wait for some Utopian future.'

I don't know where the word Utopian has come from. It has popped into my head from some weird storage box of words that I have once heard and presumed that I would never need to use. The smooth delivery of such a gem makes me feel more confident.

'Well, it's possible, you know,' Dermot replies. 'If you are desperate to see how the other half lives, you could have a sex change to become a man.'

'Don't you think that's the problem with the world?' I reply, emboldened with a newly acquired bravado. 'There are not just two halves – men and women. There are so many people not represented by that comment. There are so many people who don't feel male or female and are not comfortable being labelled as either. The world should not be divided into gender halves!'

What the hell am I talking about? I do want to be a male. I don't want to be a female. Why am I suddenly talking about those who don't want to be either? That's not me. I'm a man. I'm just hidden in this dumbass body.

Dermot is eyeing me suspiciously whilst throwing back another beer. 'Eddy never said her friend was non-binary.'

My reaction is swift and overly aggressive for the moment. 'I'm not.'

'Well, I wouldn't care if you were. I apologise for leaving out the large cohort of mankind, or "peoplekind", who do not fit into the narrow polarisation of existence we pretend is real.'

I realise that I need saving from myself. Luckily, Eddy arrives with another girl in tow.

'There you are, Ros, stop chatting up Dermot. I want you to meet Angel. She's from Brazil. She studies English with me.'

Angel is beautiful. Her hair is dark brown, and her eyes are framed with long eyelashes.

'Hi, Ros. Eddy has told me all about you. She says you want to be an engineer after secondary school.'

She has revealed my lie. My heart sinks. I have often heard that expression before, but I had never felt the full force of it until this moment. The room suddenly feels too small. I can hear my voice croak out a pathetic answer.

'Civil engineering maybe.'

'God, the gap year's a few years away, then,' Dermot says.

'Don't be an ass, Dermo, sure Ros is old in spirit,' Eddy replies, taking my arm in hers. 'She is one of us – a liberal thinker, and that's all that counts. Age is but a number.'

Angel nudges my arm gently and asks me why I would like to be an engineer.

'I don't really know,' I reply. 'It's just an answer I give to kick for touch.'

Angel looks confused. 'What does that mean, "kick for touch"?' she asks. 'My English doesn't understand everything, and I need to learn.'

'Oh, Ros is big into sports,' Eddy replies. 'It's just a sporting metaphor. I will explain it to you tomorrow in college. Time for something more interesting now.'

Eddy takes a spliff out of her back pocket and gestures to Angel for a light.

Angel produces a box of matches. 'Not for me tonight, Ed, I have a tutorial tomorrow and I need to finish my essay.'

'Just you and me then, Ros. We can release the muse together.'

I have no idea what the bloody muse is. And I am also not too sure I want to smoke weed again. My clothes stank the last time, of a sweetness that was never mine, and I had difficulty smuggling them into the wash without anyone noticing.

1.30am
Sunday
27 Beechfield Drive

I lie on my bed feeling lucky that I have escaped detection again. Ian is out for the weekend on some rugby tour and the parents are at a late-night party at the golf club – something about an Abba fancy dress evening. My mother is excited about the evening. She loves Abba and listens to them while baking. She stirs the cake mix, jiggling her body parts to 'Dancing Queen'. The thought of it makes me smile and cringe at the same time. Why are parents so embarrassing?

Although maybe I have things to be embarrassed about myself. If they only knew what I did this evening. Four beers at a student party in Rathmines is one level of mis-behaviour but smoking a spliff and going into a bedroom with a girl would be a different level of humiliation if it was discovered.

My dream of being with a girl has become a reality, but it is also turning into a nightmare. My groin aches with the thought of what I have done earlier, but my head spins with the wrongness of it all. Is that a word? Wrong-ness. Eddy would know. Eddy with the smiling eyes and beautiful body would know. She would probably laugh at my use of the word. She would also laugh that I even think that what we have done is wrong. 'We are human beings enjoying each other in ways that should be seen as normal, Ros,' she would say.

But I feel sick. I feel somehow that I have betrayed my family and their wholesome nature. Betrayed the daughter my mother thinks she has.

The unmistakable ping disturbs my negative thoughts.

I miss you.

The words of her text make everything suddenly seem right.

I miss you too.

Tonight surprised me. I didn't think you'd be so open to it. Maybe the alcohol and joint helped.

I look at her words and feel amazed that they refer to me. My behaviour has surprised me too. Where has it all come from? Maybe years of dreaming about it have helped. I think carefully about my reply and try to sound laid-back.

I don't need alcohol or drugs to do what I want to do.

Am I your first?

First what?

Are you that stoned or drunk that you've already forgotten?

But we didn't do that much.

I tingle with the thought of her naked body, her arms wrapped around me, her kisses on my neck. I am scared that I have crossed a line from which there is no return. In bed with her, I have been the person that no one else sees. I imagined being her boyfriend, taking her out, even marrying her. But I have spiralled into a future that is far from accessible in my pathetic body.

Don't shit on the moment, Ros. We did enough. Why are you being so weird about it?

I have upset her. I re-read her message. It is a question I can't answer.

Maybe I am upset that we didn't do everything. That maybe she held back because she doesn't like my body either. Maybe she is also repulsed by my lack of maleness. But that's a stupid thought. She is gay. My body is what she wants. It's just not what *I* want.

> I'm sorry. I'm just tired.

The words I type back seem pathetic. I'm not tired. I'm angry. Angry with me. My inner self hates my outer self.

Eddy doesn't accept my reply either. She is definitely pissed off with me.

> You're still in school, Ros, so I was going slow with you.

I leave the words sitting between us like heavy stones. I can't reply. She is right. I am only a bloody schoolkid, and she is in college. My eyes mist over, and I put down my phone. The screen goes dark. That's it then. There's nothing more to be written. I am a pathetic little kid who has played above their level and now the game has killed my character off and kicked me back to level one.

A little rectangle of light appears on my ceiling.

> I'm sorry Ros. I shouldn't have texted that. It doesn't bother me.

> You're less than two years older than me you know!

82

I know.

There is an awkward pause again, as I don't know what else to say to her. But she is definitely the English student. Words come easy to her.

Maybe Ros, all this is because you're not sure whether you're gay or not. And that's fine. Maybe being with me made you realise you'd prefer to be with a boy.

My reply is easy and quick.

Jesus no! I have zero interest in being with a boy, Eddy.

Really?

Yes.

I'm very happy about that of course, but why, Ros?

It doesn't matter.

Her messages go quiet then. The word 'typing' under her name disappears and I feel left with my immaturity, not knowing what to do or say next. Was my last reply too short or offensive?

But then that little word of hope reappears, and she is typing another text. I wait apprehensively for what might appear on the screen.

I'm glad it was me.

Was you?

The first to be with you naked.

How do you know you are the first?

Then tell me I'm not.

I send back a smiling emoji. And she sends back a smiling emoji with hearts for eyes.

When I read her next message, my heart feels redeemed.

> It won't be the last time,
> sweet thing.

'Rosalyn, is your light still on? You should be asleep. I hope you weren't up all night watching TikTok or whatever entertains teenagers these days.'

I can hear my father telling my mother to leave me alone. He is shushing her on the stairs. They both sound totally drunk.

'Good night, Ros.'

'Why doesn't she reply, Colin?'

'She's a teenager.'

'She's a bloody angst-driven teenager at the moment. Do you think she's having boy trouble?'

'Jesus, I can hear you, Mum. Go to bed. I'm fine.'

There are snorts of laughter from the landing and then it returns to silence as their bedroom door shuts.

> You asleep, Ros?

> No, my parents came home. They're pissed.

> Do they know?

> Know?

That you're gay.

God no. Anyway, it wouldn't be accurate.

Why? Are you bi?

Again, Jesus, no! What was the song you played tonight when we were in that bedroom?

I desperately want to change the subject. I don't want to talk about my gender or sexuality. I don't want her to have an excuse to push me away.

Which one? We played loads

It was the one playing when you were kissing me. I know you played it on purpose.

I still can't remember. Was it 'My Love Mine All Mine'?

I haven't a clue.

She sends back a laughing emoji. It is two o'clock in the morning and I want to keep talking to Eddy, but I know that in a few hours I have to get out of bed and go to a special hockey practice for our cup match next week.

> Good night, Eddy. Thank you for being my first.

> I knew it! Good night sweet thing. See you soon.

I put in my headphones and open Spotify. I need to hear the song once more to bring me back to the bedroom in Rathmines. The sweet-smelling sheets, the thick pile of books on the desk and the swivel chair covered in clothes. I look up 'My Love Mine All Mine'. It is the song.

Opening my journal, I take a pen from my bedside locker and scribble the lyrics down as quickly as I can. Then I start singing. So loudly that I am surprised that my parents don't appear at my bedroom door. But they are in the land of drunkenness and all I can hear from them is a duet of snoring.

3.20pm
Thursday
Religious Education class

It has been four days and I haven't heard anything from Eddy. I have picked up my phone and thought about texting her over the last few days, but I don't want to be the immature one, coming across as too pushy. I want her to see me as self-assured. I keep wondering what she is doing in college, who she is with, and whether she has moved on from me already.

Ray is nudging me gently. 'Ros, have you got a spare pen?'

'Why?'

'For the questions on the board!'

I haven't been paying attention. Mr Cunningham has been talking about karma for the last twenty minutes and I haven't listened to one word.

I sigh and look at the list of three questions on the whiteboard. The questions might as well be in Japanese. I have no idea how to answer them. If Sarah was still talking to me then I'd ask her. But she is sitting the other side of Ray and he doesn't usually like sharing his thoughts in class.

'Do we have to hand these in?'

'I don't know,' Ray replies. 'Why don't you ask Cunningham?'

'No, if I ask him, I might put the thought into his head. Anyway, he probably doesn't want them handed up, as it's just more correcting for him. It's not like we have an exam in this rubbish.'

Mr Cunningham is staring at me intently. 'Do you have a question about the work, Rosalyn?'

'No, sir, I was just asking Ray for a pen.'

'Hopefully he won't throw it at you,' Tadhg interjects from the back row.

There is a ripple of laughter around the room.

'I don't think that's necessary, Tadhg,' Mr Cunningham says.

'I beg to differ, sir. Isn't that exactly what karma is all about, the consequences of one's actions? Ros threw a pen in my eye and now she is being teased about it.'

The class is appreciative of Tadhg's newly acquired eloquence, but swot Jessica does not want to be overshadowed by the class troublemaker. Her hand shoots up looking for permission to speak. She gets the nod from Cunningham.

'Maybe, Tadhg, we should ask why Ros threw a pen in your eye? Maybe the pen sticking out of your eye was your karma for whatever you said to provoke her?'

The conversation is heading down a route I wish to avoid.

'But it was an accident,' I interject.

'You have the best hand-eye coordination in our year, Ros,' Jessica continues. 'So I doubt the pen in his eye was an error of your aim. He probably deserved it. It was karma!'

The class look at me. Cunningham looks at me.

'It was an accident,' Tadhg says. 'I just asked her for a lend of a pen and she turned around and threw one at me.'

'Let's get back to the questions,' Mr Cunningham implores. 'Stay quiet and answer the questions.'

But the conversation about the pen-throwing has expanded and many are not in favour of letting the opportunity to talk pass them by. Cunningham raises his voice. It booms around the room.

'NOW!'

The effect is instantaneous. The class goes quiet, and pens and paper are produced from nowhere.

Jessica is smiling at me. It's not the smile I expect. It is not the smile of someone who has thrown me under the proverbial bus, but the smile of someone who is trying to be on my side. Almost without realising it, I smile back.

However, I still don't know the answer to any of the questions on the board. I suck the end of my pen and look at the blank page in front of me. Karma. Will I reap what I have sown? I think of Eddy, the pot-smoking and her bed. Have I reaped it already?

Tadhg called me a dyke. I slept with his sister. And my karma has come back to me. I have already been in front of Viper and been given a grilling by my parents.

I hate karma!

12.40pm
Friday
Lunchroom

The queue for lunch is enormous. If I hadn't forgotten my sandwiches, standing around for twenty minutes wouldn't even be necessary. By the time I reach the top of the lunch queue, the lasagne has gone. What's left is chips and sausages or the usual healthy salads. I opt for the unhealthy, thinking I can run it off at the weekend. Not that goalies run that much.

I scan for a spare seat, but the dining room is packed. The only seats I can see empty are either with the Flock, who are munching on lettuce leaves, or with a bunch of third-year boys blowing peas at innocent victims. I head for the door.

'Hey, Rosalyn, you can squeeze in here if you like.'

Jessica looks at me from across a crowded table. I have never sat with the nerds before.

'Thanks, but there really isn't room. I'll just go outside.'

But she nudges Maddie O'Brien down the bench and wriggles over to make more space.

'There. Plenty of space for you.'

Reluctantly I sit in the gap.

'I like Mr Cunningham's classes.'

I look at Jessica and wonder what reply I should give. Rude or polite? She has always irritated me intensely. Her hair neatly brushed and tied. Her uniform immaculate.

And she doesn't roll up her sleeves or let her socks drop to her ankles.

'I'm not really interested in RE,' I say eventually.

'But you were the centre of the discussion today.'

'Yeah, thanks to you. What was all that about, Jessica?'

'Tadhg brought it up. I was just extrapolating on why you would have thrown it at him so aggressively.'

'Extrapolating? Do you always have to be so bloody smart?'

She appears hurt. 'Why do you like to play sport, Rosalyn, and win every competition you enter? That's your way to make your mark. You're good at sports. It gets you noticed. But I can't play anything to save my life, even though I try every term to get on a team. But I am clever. It's my thing. You show off in sports. I show off in class.'

'I'm not a show-off.'

'Of course you are. I've watched some of your matches. You smile at the crowd when you've made a good save. You pump your fist in the air when you've beaten an opponent.'

'That's just competitiveness.'

'Well, I'm equally competitive, but in a class situation,' she says.

'Why do you want to get on a team anyway, if you're not big into sports?'

'To be part of a group,' she says, poking her food around with a fork. 'You don't like me much, do you?' she adds.

'We don't have much in common.'

'That's because you're the female equivalent of a jock, Rosalyn. You don't care about anyone who isn't good at sports.'

'God, will you stop calling me Rosalyn. Only the teachers call me that. It's Ros.'

'Or the Beast! Why do you like that nickname? It's hardly flattering.'

My sausages and chips are not having the desired effect on my mood. I am becoming angrier by the minute.

'The name just suits me. I like being strong. I would hate to be weak and –'

She interrupts me. 'And feminine!'

There is no answer I want to give to this remark. I pick my tray up from the table and stand up.

'Don't go, Ros. I was only teasing. I'm sorry.'

I don't give her another look. I just walk away.

How dare she question my femininity! How dare she look at me and see what I refuse to tell others!

Scraping the rest of my food into the compost bin, I push my way past the other students entering for second lunch. It's cold outside, but it is preferrable to being in the dining room. Maybe I need to find Sarah and make her talk to me. I miss our friendship. I can't understand why she is still holding a grudge just because I didn't walk home with her that night. She is probably with Ray, hanging around the lockers. Her spending more time with him is making Ray very happy, but it will all come crashing down when she refuses him for the second time.

There is a distinct absence of people in the locker room. It is nearly time for the next class, but I take out my phone to see if I have missed any messages.

Mum again.

> Don't microwave the dinner for more than six minutes or you'll ruin it.

But there's also a message from Sarah.

> Ros, why didn't you sit with us at lunch? I waved at you!

I quickly type a response.

> I didn't see you. It was ridiculously full in there. I'm glad you texted me. Meet after school today?

> Sure but where are you now? We have a lecture in Moss Hall.

> Keep me a seat

> Sure. I'm with Ray. We'll keep you one

> Of course you are.

She doesn't reply, so I scan down the rest of my messages. The last one brings a smile to my face.

> Hello there

It's only two small words but it's contact. It was sent two hours ago. Hurriedly, I reply.

> Hi. How's your week been?

Way too boring. I can't send that, so I delete and start again.

> Missed you

I delete this too. Nothing needy should be sent.

> Hi Eddy, how's it going?

Jesus, pathetic. I sound like a right idiot. What do I write?

The bell for class goes. I can't afford to be late again. Stuffing the phone into my locker, I grab a pen and paper and head for Moss Hall.

The reply will have to wait until later.

4.10pm
Friday
Eccleston Road

The nearly dark November afternoon is chilly. I can see my breath as I walk. There is a stream of students in front of us heading for the DART.

'I hate this time of year. Dark going to school and dark going home. It's like we miss whole days of our lives just stuck in school.'

'More like months,' Sarah says.

'Years.'

We laugh.

It has been a week since we have done something so simple together as chat and laugh. I grab the opportunity of her lighter mood.

'I'm sorry for not walking home with you from the party.'

Sarah smiles at me. 'Really? I hope so. I was so damned scared, Ros. You know how spooked I get at any shadows or footsteps. I didn't walk home. I ran.'

'You should really stop watching programmes like *Stranger Things*. They just frighten you.'

'Well, I was bloody running up that hill when I thought there was a guy following me past the old house on Ludlow roundabout.'

'Very funny. I see what you did there!'

Sarah heaves her schoolbag on to her other shoulder to spread the pain of carrying the heavy books.

'I thought we were not going to have to do this in TY. I thought there were going to be no flipping textbooks to lug around.'

'It's just because you're so short. We do have far fewer books than last year.'

She gives me a dirty look, but it is not an angry one. 'Well, this English textbook is so massive it makes up for all the others we didn't need to buy.'

I smile at her and take the bag from her shoulder. 'I can carry it if you like.'

'You don't have to do that, Ros. I accept your apology. I was just hurt that you left me like that. You've never done it before. And BFFs don't do that. But then you've been acting a bit strange lately.'

'I have not.'

Sarah stops and turns to look at me. 'It's fine, you know.'

'What's that supposed to mean?'

'Ros, we've been best friends since we were little. I've grown up with you. But we've grown up into very different people.'

My chest is seizing, and my breath sticks behind a lump in my throat.

'Ros, are you OK? I'm not trying to upset you. But I'm not the only one who sees this. We all do.'

'Who is the "we", Sarah? And what do they think they know?'

My mind is racing, and I wonder if Eddy has told Tadhg about us. Her brother would be only too happy to spread it around the year. I feel sick. I don't want people to know. And I don't want them knowing something that isn't even the truth, finding the wrong me in all this chaos.

'All your close friends – Cassie, Ray, Beth. Although after that party, others are questioning it too.'

I kick a stone from the pavement on to the road, narrowly missing a cyclist.

'I don't know why you're so angry about this, Ros. It's not a big issue these days.'

The lump in my throat is now choking me. I can feel tears in my eyes.

'Because I'm not bloody gay, Sarah. I'm not a "lezzer".'

The words blurt out aggressively.

Sarah grabs my arm and pulls me towards her for a hug. 'But it's OK if you are.'

I push her away and wipe a tear from my eye. 'So, what is it about me that makes you think I'm gay? Is it because I'm not your stereotypical airhead that behaves like the Flock? Because if that's the problem, you don't get spray tans or wear make-up either, Sarah.'

She looks decidedly uneasy. 'I'm sorry, Ros, I shouldn't have said anything. But I thought we could tell each other everything.'

'I'm not a lesbian, Sarah.'

'OK, OK. I believe you.'

But I'm too incensed to drop the subject. 'So why does everybody think I am? It's not bloody fair. It's gender stereotyping. I hate the fact that you've been talking about me behind my back. That's disloyal.'

'I'm not disloyal, Ros. I just care and so do the others. We're your friends! And after the problems you had before you came to first year. It's just – you seem to be going back there.'

I throw her bag to the floor. 'I wish I'd never told you about any of that.'

'You're being unfair, Ros. And this is just like you these days. You're so angry about everything. Why do you think you're called the Beast? Do you really think it's because you're strong? It's not. It's because you'd drill a ball through anyone who gets in your way on the pitch. You can be vicious.'

Her words are difficult to hear.

'Some bloody friend you are, accusing me of being gay and now accusing me of being too aggressive.'

'Well, why are you so angry with everything, then?'

I look at Sarah and I know I'm showing that same anger.

'I didn't know being angry was a sign of being gay.'

Sarah picks up her bag from the pavement. 'Jesus, it's not just that, Ros.'

'So what is it, then?'

Sarah shrugs her shoulders. 'I don't want to fight like this, Ros. We're supposed to be friends.'

'Then just tell me why you think I'm gay.'

'Why does it matter, Ros, if you say you're not?'

'It matters to me. So please tell me.'

'OK. But you asked, remember that.'

'Just tell me.'

'OK. You never wear skirts or dresses, except your school skirt. You hate make-up and girly stuff. You don't date boys. You don't even talk about them except to say you've beaten one at pool. And when we had that last sex education class with Shirley, you kept asking about gays and transgender and non-binary people. It was as if it mattered more to you than it did to the rest of us.'

The road is quiet except for our voices. The trail of students has gone, dispersed into awaiting cars or jammed on to the DART.

And we go quiet too. Aware that we are out in the open, being too visible in our disagreement. Everything Sarah has said is true, but all those things don't add up to someone being gay. I repeat the statement I have already made, but this time slowly and without aggression.

'I'm not gay.' It is a closing statement. It doesn't require a reply or more conversation on the topic.

She nods and turns towards the DART station, and we begin walking. 'I'm sorry, Ros.'

'It's OK, Sarah. Forget it.'

The DART is Friday-afternoon full. There are very few seats left and people are standing in the doorways, chatting or staring into phones. I brush past the throng and find a single seat beside an old woman holding a shopping bag on her knees. Usually, I would stand and chat to Sarah about the day. But I am in no mood for further conversation. Unzipping my bag, I take out my phone.

Eddy's simple text is still unanswered. I have no idea what to reply. And maybe I shouldn't reply at all if everyone is already assuming that I'm gay. Maybe I should leave the two words unanswered, my silence sending a message of its own.

Little dots appear on the screen. She is typing.

> Hello there again. You must be finished school by now.

I hate that she mentions school. I want to be in college, with her. I want to be reading Hardy and writing essays on the romanticism of his poetry. I want to be in her bed, holding her tightly, feeling her breath on my neck.

But I want to be dead too.

The last thought shocks me. It has surfaced from my subconscious. Is that what I really wish for? To cease to exist? Although knowing my bloody luck, I'd end up in Nirvana with a pile of Hindus waiting to be reincarnated as a monk – or a slug.

Without thinking of my surroundings, I roll up my sleeve and look at the scars on my lower arm. One hasn't healed and is still seeping. They are the anger Sarah mentioned. They are the self-hatred, my hatred of my stupid body, which keeps me in a life I hate.

Why wasn't I born as Ian? Why didn't my father's sperm and my mother's egg produce another son?

In biology class, Ms Jackson said it is the sperm that decides the sex of a baby. Maybe my father produced a defective sperm, a sperm unsure of itself, one that swam up and just created chaos. Although maybe this life is my karma for being a bad man in a past life?

Cunningham's religion class has obviously affected me at some level. Ridiculous. What am I doing, thinking about having more than one life? But I can't help wondering if I have lived before, in the body of a man. Are these ridiculous breasts and monthly blood-lettings caused by my behaviour in a whole other time? It says so much about what I feel about being female that I think my femininity is a curse.

The old woman beside me is tutting under her breath. She is looking at my uncovered arm. Quickly I pull down my sleeve and turn to look out the window.

My thoughts are still fuelled by anger. Bloody gay! I wish I was. That would be much easier. At least I would like my own body then. At least I would be able to stand up and say, *This is who I am*, without people thinking I'm deranged. Sometimes it feels like that. Sometimes it feels like I'm mad. Society has males and females, and my body is female, so why does my brain try to convince me that I'm male? Is my brain malfunctioning? Because no matter how many of my physical attributes deny me a masculine existence, I still believe I'm male.

I know loads of gay people. It seems acceptable. Even rational. But I don't know one transgender or non-binary person, except for those I see on TV. And none of them is like me. They are all MTF – male to female. They are all extremely feminine in their clothes and appearance. They exaggerate their existence, as if ramping up the excess will convince people of their trans nature.

My phone pings.

> What do you want for your birthday?

>> What do you mean? I've already had my birthday!

> Yes. But I missed it. And I don't want to wait another year to buy you a present.

I do know what I want, and I reply without caring what Eddy thinks of my forwardness.

>> I want to see you.

Her reply is quick.

> Great. I have a free house this weekend. Tadhg is playing a tournament in Cork and Mum and Dad are going to watch the borefest! We can celebrate your birthday here!

The idea dissipates all my anger.

And listen to music?

If that's a euphemism for something else, then of course.

I can feel my face blush as I read her message.

What's your favourite food, sweet thing? I'll cook.

I don't really have a favourite. I eat anything.

Pick one!

OK. Thai. I love massaman curry.

She sends three laughing emojis.

I don't think I've ever cooked that, but I will give it a try.

Don't bother. We can order pizza.

Nope. I'm cooking.

What time will I arrive?

There is a pause in the messages.

Come over in the afternoon. We can listen to music first! Say two o'clock?

Perfect.
Thanks, Eddy.

6.30pm
Friday
27 Beechfield Drive

My father is patting Ian on the back and smiling like a loon.

'I am so proud of you, Ian. I just can't express how happy I am. To be the captain of the under-21s is such an achievement.'

Ian is tucking into his steak and chips, so his reply comes between mouthfuls. 'To be honest, Dad, it's going to be a tough tournament. And Jeggers had to call off. He pulled a hamstring in our last practice. He's gutted.'

My mother, eager to be part of the rugby conversation, lets out a sigh. 'Oh, that sounds awful, poor Jonathan. Will he be out for long?'

'Don't know, Ma, difficult to say yet. But he's a great loss. He's a powerhouse at the back of the pack.'

My mother shakes her head. My father meanwhile has thought of the relevant question to ask. 'So who's replacing him as number eight?'

'Tadhg Morrisey. You know, the guy Ros hit in the eye with a pen.'

I wince, but everyone ignores my sensitivities.

Ian continues as if I don't exist except as a target for his teasing. 'He's a cracking player for his age and he's built like a brickhouse.'

'You've got a good team. Your mum and I can't wait to watch the tournament.'

My mother gives me a pleading look. 'We wish you'd come too, Ros. We hate leaving you behind.'

'I have my own training tomorrow, Mum. I can't miss it. We've a league match next week.'

My mother sighs, as only she can do when I've disappointed her. 'But we'd prefer to have you with us than sitting here home alone.'

'I won't be home alone. I'm going out with friends to the cinema tomorrow and pizza afterwards. So it's all good.'

My father reaches into his pocket and takes out fifty euro. 'Well, take this, honey, and you can pay for the pizzas.'

'Thanks, Dad.'

My mother is less easy to placate. 'Do you want me to call Beth and ask her can you spend the weekend with them? I hate seeing you home by yourself, and if you're going to the cinema with Sarah anyway...'

My mum is a constant fixer. She can never let things go without having some influence on the outcome of events. I give her my most persuasive look.

'No thanks, Mum. I'm looking forward to having the TV all to myself on Saturday night and I really don't need anyone supervising me any more.'

My father reaches over and squeezes my hand. 'You may be seventeen, Rosalyn, but you will always be my little girl.'

Underneath my jumper, my arm is stinging.

2.30pm
Saturday
The Lodge

The door opens and Eddy smiles at me. She is holding a pen in her hand.

'Perfect timing. I've just finished writing your birthday card.'

'I don't need a card.'

'Nonsense. I told you, I want to celebrate the birthday I just missed. I want to celebrate you.'

She smiles at me, and I grin back at her. I follow her into the kitchen. On the table is a present wrapped in heart-covered paper, and there is an envelope stuck to the outside.

'This is for you,' she says, picking up the gift from the table.

'You shouldn't have.'

'Oh, I had to. Lewis Carroll says, "There are three hundred and sixty-four days when you get un-birthday presents and only one for birthday presents," so I didn't want to miss the opportunity. Please open it.'

Carefully I unwrap the sheet of paper. The face on the sleeve of the vinyl record is young and long-haired and one that I don't recognise. I read aloud the writing above the image.

'Van Morrison, *Astral Weeks*.'

'Look at the back, Ros. The third track.'

'"Sweet Thing"!'

Eddy takes my hand and pulls me towards her. The kiss is long and beautiful.

'Happy birthday, Ros!'

'It's the best present, Eddy. Thank you.'

'Would you like to go upstairs and listen to music?'

I can feel my face turn red. It gives away my innocence. The words are missing, but I nod. Without speaking, we go up the circular stairs, past the photographs of her family on the landing wall.

Her room is the same as I remember from the party. There are bookshelves of novels, a desk with an open laptop and cushion covers on a couch in the corner. The covers are printed with an image of a woman with a unibrow and red lipstick.

'I meant to ask you last time. What's with the strange cushions?'

Eddy laughs. 'Don't you know who she is?'

'I haven't a clue.'

'It's my favourite artist – Frida Kahlo.'

'Never heard of her.'

'Well, I will tell you all about her another time. Now I would prefer to listen to music than talk about Frida.' She pats the duvet.

With anticipation of the gift I really want, I sit down beside her.

The sun is streaming through the bedroom window and lighting up the room. I feel I'm older. Not just seventeen but more mature. And I'm no longer innocent.

'I'm glad you're only a year and a bit younger than me,' Eddy says, brushing her hand gently over my cheek.

'And you are only a year and a bit older,' I laugh.

'Idiot.'

'But I don't care about age, Eddy. It's nothing. I just hate being in school when you're in college.'

Eddy winces slightly. 'You made that obvious at the party. You didn't have to pretend to be on a gap year. My friends are chilled. They wouldn't care whether or not you were in school. I think Dermot was trying to chat you up until he found out you lied to him. He's an ethics student in more than just his degree.'

'I feel bad about that. Did they all talk about me and how much of an ass I am?'

'Not really. Not the ass bit anyway. They just asked where we had met and how long we'd been together.'

'Are we together, Eddy? Don't you mind being with a TY student?'

'If I kiss you like this, will that convince you that I don't mind?'

Eddy rolls over on top of me and starts kissing my neck and face. I want her to stop and seriously answer my question. I don't want to be with her now and be discarded a few weeks later. But it is difficult to stop something that makes me feel so happy. I'm with a girl. I'm living my dream. All those nights lying in my bed, practice-kissing my hand, pretending to be male, are dreams with substance now.

'Ros, please take your T-shirt off. I think we're past being shy now.'

Reluctantly, I pull away. 'Do you mind if I don't? I would like to take it slowly.'

She sighs and reaches for her phone. 'You're a funny one, sweet thing, fast in some ways and slow in others. What music would you like to listen to on your belated birthday?'

'I don't know. Something you love. Something I haven't heard from your playlist.'

She looks thoughtful and then smiles. 'I know just the song.'

A strumming guitar with a soft percussion starts.

'That's beautiful.'

'Do you know who it is?'

'Not a clue. But I think I've heard my brother listening to it.'

'You're not big into music, are you?'

'Not really. I prefer sport. Is that a problem?'

Eddy holds my hand in hers and starts rubbing my fingers gently. 'Not at all, I can educate you. It will be fun. I can educate you in music – and other things.'

'Well, before all my education, do you think we could eat? I'm starving.'

The kitchen is beautifully warm, thanks to a large range cooker emitting heat. Eddy points to a high stool at the island and hands me a beer.

'Sit here and have a drink while I cook dinner.'

'Are you really going to cook for me?'

'I'm not just going to cook for you. I'm going to lay on the whole package. Drink, dinner and a birthday cake.'

Eddy takes some off-white substance from the fridge and starts cutting it into cubes.

'What's that?'

She cuts more cubes. 'It's tofu. I can't handle or cut meat. So you'll have to be vegan like me for the night. Sorry, I suppose I should have asked you first. Do you mind?'

'It depends on what it tastes like.'

'Fair enough. But it doesn't really taste like anything. It needs flavour added to it, so it works well in curries.'

We talk as she cooks. And watching her, I realise that she is even more beautiful than I first noticed. She smiles more than anyone else I have ever met, and her smile is wide and almost cheeky.

'You do realise you're staring at me,' she says.

'I have nothing else to do, and you're beautiful.' I know I am blushing again as I say the words, but I want her to know.

'Will you tell your parents that you have a beautiful new girlfriend, then?'

Her words break the illusion.

In my mind, we are in a different reality. We are boyfriend and girlfriend, enjoying each other's company, a thousand light years from 27 Beechfield Drive. I have created a parallel universe in my mind that I can keep away from the rest of my life. It will be stored in one of my safe boxes and tucked away with the Ark of the Covenant when I have to go back into the reality of being Ros.

Talking about my parents shatters my fragile new universe.

'I won't tell them.'

Eddy pours some coconut milk over the paste in the frying pan. 'That's sad. Are you ashamed to be with me?'

'No. It's just that I don't talk to my parents about anything in my personal life. We don't have that kind of relationship. I'm a quiet person at home.'

I'm lying. It is all about shame. I would be ashamed of sleeping with a girl and pretending to be a gay person. I would be ashamed of being seen as a lesbian when I am not and can't be a lesbian, because I am not a woman. It is all so complicated.

'I think you're quiet in every situation,' Eddy says.

Looking at how relaxed she is with the conversation, I am overcome with a frightening thought. 'Will you tell your parents about me?'

'Well, usually I would tell them if I'm serious about someone, so I won't be telling them yet.'

She sees the disappointment on my face. Touching my nose playfully with the end of the wooden spoon, she smiles at me again.

'I'm teasing, Ros. I don't tell them about my relationships either.'

'That's good. Your brother is in my class, and I can't face being called a dyke in school again.'

Eddy's mood darkens. 'Don't use that word, Ros. It's a slur on people like you and me. It makes our relationship dirty when it's not.'

Her outburst reveals a fragility. I create my reply carefully.

'I'm sorry. I understand. I hate that word too.'

Eddy stops stirring the pan and walks around the island towards me. She hugs me tightly and whispers in my ear. 'It's a word that has done a lot of damage to me.'

Without saying anything more she points to the long scar on her arm, the one she had told me was from a car accident.

'It was no accident,' she says softly now. 'I was in third year in school. I felt happy to be me, so I came out to someone I loved. I stupidly thought because I accepted who I was back then, everyone else would. I was naive. They wrote *DYKE* on my locker in large black letters and bullied me incessantly. It doesn't matter what we are taught in wellbeing class, kids are still homophobic. College is so much better. No-one gives a fuck. You can be who you are and sleep with who you like.'

Her swearing jars. She is always in control of her emotions, but this memory is clearly still raw.

'So you did this to yourself?' I ask, touching the scar gently.

'Will you think less of me if I say yes?'

I shake my head. 'Of course not. I understand.'

'Do you remember the song I played for you in bed?'

The mellow voice and gentle music is easy to recall.

'Yes. I do. It was sad. Although appropriate for my birthday, I suppose.'

She starts singing. Her voice is soft and as good as the artist on the Spotify track.

I try to say something, but she continues singing.

When the song is over, she looks deflated.

'They're beautiful lyrics, aren't they? It's called "At Seventeen". We do cheat ourselves into thinking someone will want us for who we are, the ugly girls staying at home, playing solitaire and never getting Valentine's Day cards.'

'But you're not ugly, Eddy. That song's not you.'

'But my sexuality was deemed ugly. And I have spent a lot of time at home inventing people to be in my life. Coming out is not always the best move to make when you're young.'

We eat dinner at a long oak table. I am ageing again as we eat. I have never had a meal with a romantic partner before. And there are wine glasses and a bottle of pro-secco, making me feel that I am so far out of my comfort zone that I am inhabiting a dream. I feel twenty-seven, not seventeen.

'This is delicious.'

'Even the tofu?'

'Especially the tofu,' I respond.

'Well, I've never made a massaman before, so I'm glad you're enjoying it. Thank goodness for those little jars of paste, though. I found it this morning when I went to buy your cake. I'm afraid I didn't have time to make a cake myself.'

'I didn't expect one.'

'I'm sorry about my mood earlier. That word just brought back tough times.'

She is smiling, but her eyes look sad.

'Did you do it with a razor blade or a knife?'

'God, Ros, that's a very gory question.'

I roll up my sleeve and show her the cuts on my arm. 'This is why I asked you. And why I wouldn't take my shirt off in bed. I'm embarrassed about them.'

She takes my arm in her hand and starts kissing the line of little scars; scars that are closely inflicted to be more easily hidden.

'What a stupid pair we are.'

'Yes, but you're smarter than me, Eddy. You've stopped doing it. You have, Eddy, haven't you?'

I look pleadingly into her eyes. I want her to be the rock on which I can depend, the outcome I can achieve one day. I want to be like her, proud of my existence.

She puts down her fork and takes a sip of water. 'I only did it once, Ros, because I hurt myself so badly.'

'Who was the person you told?'

'A girl in my year. We were friends, but I fell in love with her. One day we were at her house, and we sneaked cider into her bedroom. We got drunk and I made a pass at her. She was horrified and pushed me out of her room. I felt disgusting. I went home and attacked myself with a kitchen knife. I blacked out and woke up in a puddle of blood. My mother screamed when she saw my arm. I was sent off for a whole month of therapy. But the girl told everyone in class what had happened and then the bullying started.'

'Oh god, Eddy, that's so awful. Do you still see her at all?'

'She was at the party in Rathmines.'

'Which one was she?'

'It doesn't matter. It was a long time ago.'

'Is she one of your gay friends?'

'No. She went out with Dermot for the last two years of school. But she did something recently which made me wonder.'

Eddy stands up and walks out of the kitchen. I don't know whether I'm supposed to follow her or stay and finish my dinner. But she returns quickly, with a book in her hand.

'She gave me this two weeks ago. I don't suppose you know it?'

I take the book from her hand and look at the title and author. Caitlin Moran, *How to Build a Girl*. Of course I've never heard of it. I hardly read anything.

'Is it good?' I ask, trying to be interested.

'It's a quite filthy coming-of-age novel. It came with a card saying that it was a pity we were all so insecure in school. She signed it "The bitch who outed you because she felt something too".'

She takes the novel from my hand and opens a well-thumbed page.

Slowly she reads out a short section.

'"Self-harm – the world will come at you with knives anyway. You do not need to beat them to it."'

'So, she knows about your arm?'

Eddy nods. 'I told her at our graduation party. There we were, all tarted up in our dresses and high-heeled shoes, and I showed her my arm in a drunken moment. I made her feel bad about herself. It was my revenge. But, in our drunken state, we both cried, and we became friends again.'

'Do you still fancy her?'

'Oh god, sweet thing, that's not why I showed you the book or read out the piece. I wasn't trying to make you jealous. I wanted to tell you because, when I was in therapy, the same sentence that she underlined in the book was scrawled on the toilet wall outside the office. Isn't that the strangest synchronicity? The universe must want me to remember the message – to be kind and love myself, because there are enough people out there who would harm me.'

'I wouldn't harm you, Eddy.'

She gives me a wry smile.

'Unfortunately, Ros, there are no certainties in life. Especially in love. But as Tennyson said, "'Tis better to have loved and lost than never to have loved at all."'

11.45am
Saturday
Dundrum Shopping Centre

The concourse is heaving with people, some tugging children behind them, all armed with shopping bags. Carol singers are bellowing out 'Deck the Halls' and rattling buckets for a good cause. Sarah and Ray have gone to look for a present for his mother. They have become very close. I'm not jealous of their 'friendship' – it keeps Sarah from noticing my absences with Eddy. I've told them I will meet them later, as this is my opportunity to find something for Eddy for Christmas. We've decided to put a limit to our spending, so I've made a list of what is possible with twenty euro. But it's difficult, as I want it to be romantic. It's not that I'm a particularly romantic person. I never have been. But Eddy is. And I want her to have that romance reciprocated.

I find myself standing in Eason's, surrounded by likeminded people who also think a book is a good present. The latest titles are disappearing from the shelves and there is too much jostling for me to take my time and browse through the offers.

Besides, Eddy wouldn't want a modern novel. I should buy her a classic. The problem is that I have been in her bedroom, and she already has shelves sagging with stories from the classic authors. Maybe I should just give up. There are still four weeks to Christmas.

'Didn't have you down as a reader.'

A bearded person to my right is smiling at me. For a moment I don't recognise him. He now has more piercings and a tattoo over his eyebrow.

'Paddy, long time no see.'

I don't know what else to say. Although he has been in my year at school, we have never really talked.

'Yes, I've been avoiding education. Well, that's not entirely true. I've been avoiding institutionalised learning. I'm still in education, but at home with online support.'

'You didn't win the board over with your petition then?'

He picks up a book from the shelf and puts it into my hand. 'Win or lose, I never wanted to go back to that den of indoctrination anyway. They're just moulding us to be puppets of the system.'

'You'd get on well with Eamonn Walters, he thinks the same.'

Paddy smiles again, and behind all the facial hair his smile is wide and friendly.

'Ah, Eamo and I are good mates. We rant about the Republic of Shite every week. Our country's a disgrace – high fuel costs, rentals through the roof, nowhere for people to live. There's not much hope for our generation in this mess. We'll just become the next diaspora.'

I am stunned by his political opinions. I have zilch. I'm never interested in what is going on in the news, especially if it is politically based. My family never talk about such things at dinner. In our house, it's all sport, mostly golf and rugby, and possibly hockey if I join in the conversation.

I look at the book he has thrust into my hand – *A Scandalous Life: The Biography of Jane Digby.*

'Why are you giving me this?'

'Because it's worth reading,' he replies. 'Personally, I love non-fiction. Books about people who don't fit into the mould. People who push the envelope. This Victorian woman is all about pushing back against the societal norms of her time.'

I feel immature in his presence. He is the same age, but he seems lightyears older.

'I've a friend who would love you, Paddy. She has the same passion for books.'

'And you don't?'

I begin to feel shallow about my likes and dislikes. 'I know I should read more but it's finding the time.'

'Yes, you're big into sport, aren't you? You're the Beast of hockey.'

When he says my nickname, it doesn't sound impressive.

'I do love playing sports but it's important to develop other interests too.'

What the hell am I saying? Am I trying to impress a school dropout who likes odd books on Victorian women?

'Well, start developing with Mary Lovell then.'

'Who?'

He takes the book from my hand and points out the author's name on the cover. I feel even more stupid. But he hasn't meant it rudely. I can see that he has no desire to insult me.

'It really is a good book. Jane Digby's life was amazing. She divorced an English lord, slept with the King of Bavaria, and then shocked the whole of British society by running off to Syria where she married a Muslim Bedouin, twenty years younger. How radical is that for the time she lived in? The woman is a legend!'

I look at the ash-white face on the cover. I'm starting to feel a sense of admiration for Jane Digby, although I know nothing about her apart from what Paddy has just told me.

'So are you going to buy it? Have I persuaded you?'

'Probably not. It's twenty-four euro.'

He seems disappointed. 'Never mind. I tried.'

He places *A Scandalous Life* back on the shelf. 'Better keep looking for a book for my dad. See you around, Rosalyn.'

'It's Ros.'

But he hasn't heard me. He is walking away towards the autobiographies.

I watch him leave. He is dressed in a pair of old denims and a long raincoat which almost touches his knees. He looks like one of Eddy's friends rather than a contemporary of mine. When he has gone from sight, I turn back to the bookshelf and pick up a copy of *A Scandalous Life*.

Maybe it is the right book for Eddy. Maybe she will be impressed if I choose a biography full of dangerous liaisons.

I find Sarah and Ray sitting at a table sucking the same smoothie from a plastic cup.

'You'll never guess who I bumped into in Eason's?'

'Nicki Minaj.'

I shake my head. 'Don't be daft, Sarah.'

'I'm not. She's in Dublin for a concert.'

Ray stops sucking at the smoothie to join the conversation. 'We should have got tickets. I'd love to see her.'

There is a lull as a young waitress arrives with our three paninis.

'We ordered your favourite, toasted ham and cheese with no relish.'

'Thanks, guys. How much do I owe you?'

'Oh, Ray paid for everything.'

'That's your Christmas present, Ros,' Ray says through a mouthful of breakfast panini.

'No, really, Ray, I'd prefer to pay.'

But Sarah tugs my sleeve. 'Let him pay, Ros. Anyway, you never told us who you saw in Eason's.'

'Paddy.'

'Paddy who?'

'Paddy Fitz, who used to be in our class.'

Sarah rolls her eyes. 'God, he's meant to have turned into a right arse. Seemingly he hangs around with Eamonn. They are probably planning a mass shooting.'

I am surprised by how negative she is, but then Sarah prefers people to behave within the boundaries of her understanding. She has always found anyone outside of the box strangely intimidating.

'He was actually really friendly and nice.'

'God, you do surprise me. Tadhg's crew adore him because he's so anti everything. And of course, the Flock love him as he's meant to be hot, but I think he's a bit full of himself. Does he still have perfect hair?'

I laugh at her question. 'Yes, he does. But he also has a beard and a moustache. Honestly, he looks more like a college student than one of us.'

'I like him.'

Sarah and I look suspiciously at Ray.

'Duh, no! Not *like* him, like that. I just mean he's an OK bloke. To be honest, so's Eamonn. I would prefer to hang out with them than Tadhg's lot any day.'

Sarah puts her arm around Ray's shoulder. 'That's because you're so sweet. You're not a jock in any way. Which is why we love you.'

Ray blushes slightly and Sarah seems happy that she has made him blush.

'So, what's in the bag, Ros? What book did you buy?' asks Sarah.

I stumble slightly over my words, trying to think of a suitable answer.

'I bought a present for my mum.'

'Ooh, show us,' Ray says. 'If it's good I might get it for my mum. We found nothing. It's hard. She likes so little.'

He lifts my Eason's bag off the floor and takes out the book before I can stop him.

'*A Scandalous Life: The Biography of Jane Digby.* Is your mum into this kind of stuff? Mine would prefer chick lit, I think.'

I take the book off him and return it to its bag. 'The shop assistant said it was a great read. It's about a Victorian woman who marries an Arab in Syria.'

'Dope. Sounds mad. I'm sure your mum will love it.' But the look on Ray's face says the total opposite.

The three of us burst out laughing.

'I know,' I add. 'It does look a bit highbrow for Mum.'

'It looks a bit risqué,' Sarah says. 'Maybe you should take it back and change it for something else.'

Ray stands up. 'I'm off to the jacks. The film starts in twenty minutes – if we're still going.'

He walks away and Sarah puts her hand on mine.

'I'm glad you came out with us today.'

'Why wouldn't I?'

'You know why, Ros. We've been a bit off with each other lately. Look, I'm sorry for saying what I did.'

'What? Calling your best friend a lesbian? Nothing against lesbians, but I'm not one.'

'Are we still best friends?' she asks.

'Of course. So are you shifting Ray?'

She smiles. 'Yes I am.'

'I just knew you two would get together.'

'What do you think?' she asks.

'He's cool. A bit of a puppy, but sweet.'

6.30pm
Saturday
Rathmines

The room is cold. I sit on the bed in my coat. It is where we have met the last six times, but I still feel awkward sitting here without Eddy. The room belongs to Maisie, Eddy's friend with the big green eyes and beautiful face. She goes home to Cork every weekend and leaves Eddy her key, so we can hang out together undisturbed.

I stand up and walk to the desk covered in college books. An essay is lying across a pile of printed notes.

I pick it up, but I can't even understand the title. There is no way I could study philosophy.

Eddy walks through the door and dumps a bag of shopping on the sofa.

'Sorry about that, sweet thing. I thought we shouldn't drink all of Maisie's beer. Have you been waiting long?'

'No, I've just arrived. Thanks for leaving the key.'

'No problem. I was hoping to get back before you but there was a huge queue in the shop. But never mind all that. Come here and kiss me.'

It never fails to turn my stomach into a mess of knots. The thought of being with her always leaves me stricken. 'I've missed you this week,' she says, taking off her coat and untying her shoelaces, 'so don't just stand there smiling at me like some idiot. Start stripping.'

I blush. She is always more forward than me. Always more assured.

'Maybe you need some of this to help you relax.' Eddy holds out a joint she has taken from her back pocket.

'No thanks. I told you I was as sick as a dog last time.'

'I don't think that was the weed, silly. I think it was the neat vodka. I did warn you not to drink so quickly.'

'You think I'm immature, Eddy.'

She pulls me over to the bed and sits me down.

'Don't be daft, Ros.'

'But I know so little. And you know everything!'

She puts a finger to my lips and gently eases me back on the bed.

'And I would exchange all of my book knowledge to know you more,' she says, laying a kiss on my cheek.

'Don't tease me, Eddy. I'm serious.'

'Well, you shouldn't be so serious. You should just enjoy what is here in front of you and stop worrying about things. You're such a worrier. You and I are different, but I love our differences, Ros. I love that you always hang up your coat rather than throwing it on the floor like I do. I love that you read things aloud without even realising you're doing it. And I love the way I feel when you kiss me.'

I'm smiling now. 'You like the way I kiss you?'

'Yes. And I like the way you hold me in your arms when we fall asleep together.'

'I like that too.'

She rolls over and lifts herself on to her elbows, looking down at me.

'I have a new song I think you'd like. Well, it's not a new song but it's a beautiful song from way back.'

'Don't tell me, from the eighties again!'

She takes out her phone and connects it to the speaker on the desk. 'No, it's even further back than that. It's seventies.'

'My grandmother must know it then.'

She digs me in the ribs and plays the music. She always sings along.

'Do you know it?' she asks.

I start laughing. 'No, obviously not. I never know your old music.'

'You don't know any of my latest favourites either! But do you like this song?'

'I like you singing it.'

She kisses me and the song keeps going without her accompanying it.

When the track finishes, she looks at me. 'You have to love those lyrics.'

'What's the song called?'

'It's perfectly titled for this moment, Ros. It's called "Love and Affection". The singer is an icon in her community.'

But I don't really care whether she's a Nobel prize winner because I want to go back to kissing. I want the feeling in my groin to return. But I know that the music matters to Eddy, so I ask her why the singer is so important.

'She was a feminist icon way back before most black women made it big in music. She writes all her own songs.

Started when she was fourteen. And best of all, she's a lesbian.'

'Does that matter?' I shouldn't have said it. I'm never going to get kissed now.

Eddy is sitting up and launching into a full rant on the importance of having lesbian icons in society. There have been male gay icons for centuries, but lesbians have had to work harder to become accepted.

I take her word for it. I know very little about lesbianism.

'And you also know the music of another well-known lesbian musician. Remember "At Seventeen"?'

'Do you only listen to lesbian singers?'

'Of course not, but these women way back then were pushing the envelope, trail blazing. Today it's easier to be yourself but they had to fight for acceptance.'

But I interrupt her with a change of subject. 'I bought you a Christmas present today.'

She smiles at me. 'Can I see it?'

'Of course not, it's not Christmas yet.'

'Well, you can give it to me the night of the party.'

'What party?'

'My parents are holding a Christmas party this year to celebrate twenty-one years of married bliss or something equally cringy, but they've said that we can have a few friends there too. I want you to come. Maisie, Dermot and Jack are all coming.'

There is no way that I want to be at that party, but I don't know how to tell her without upsetting her.

'When is it?'

'The twenty-third.'

I try to look disappointed. 'Oh, that's a pity. I won't be able to make it that day. My family always go to my grandparents on the twenty-third.'

Eddy looks sad.

'But anyway, Eddy, how could I come as your friend with Tadhg there?'

'He's not going to be there. I wouldn't have asked you if he was. He's off skiing with some other bozo in your class. Some new friend of his. Carl, I think he said.'

'What? Carl Flynn? I didn't think Tadhg would give him the time of day. He's not usually one of his crew.'

'What can I say, he's probably only friends because Carl's parents have a chalet in Courcheval. He's shallow, my brother, easily bought.'

Damn it, I could have gone to the party. I should have waited and not been so quick to refuse. Now I am stuck in a fictitious family get-together when I could be spending time with Eddy.

'Won't you give me some clue about my present?' she begs. 'Pretty please.'

I remain strong. 'Absolutely not. Presents must be a surprise.'

'I totally disagree. Why do they call them "presents" if you can't have them now?'

'Bloody English student. Think you're so smart.'

'And I am, Ros, very smart indeed.'

'And why's that?'

'Because I know you're lying about the twenty-third. You looked panicked when I asked you, so you made up some cock-and-bull story about your family. You were afraid of bumping into Tadhg.'

I let out a tell-tale sigh.

'See, I'm right. You've no family thing at all.'

'So can I come to your parents' party after all?'

She leans over to the bedside table and takes the remainder of the joint and lights it.

'I will think about it, sweet thing. I will think about it. Anyway, you just might get invited to another party in my house soon after.'

I take the joint from her and pull slowly. I am still nervous about its effect on me. 'What do you mean, another party?'

'Tadhg's convinced my parents to let him have a New Year's Eve party for being chosen for some bloody rugby team or other. It looks like he's inviting a cast of thousands, so you might make the list. I think he's forgiven you for the pen thing now. But maybe you won't be coming to that one, as I won't be there.'

I look at her, confused.

'Oh I really don't care, sweet thing. I know you're new to all this and being out there scares you. I have other plans for that night, as I said, but no reason you shouldn't go to his party if you want to.'

She is taking long drags now and waving her free hand in the air as if conducting some imaginary orchestra.

'Are you stoned already, Eddy? Oh, look at me, I'm rhyming my words!'

'Then maybe you're the one stoned. Do you know what Maya Angelou, Quentin Tarantino and Jack Kerouac all have in common?'

'I don't even know who they are.'

She doesn't seem impressed. 'They all smoked weed, sweet thing. They all took the whacky tobacky. It's the muse of many a genius.'

'And you're going to be the next genius, are you?'

'Why not!'

'Because too much of this stuff can be dangerous. I've a cousin who has fried his brain with marijuana.'

'Jesus, Ros, you sound like my mum.'

'I just don't want that for you, Eddy.'

'You're too serious, Ros. It's not like I'm addicted or anything. Lighten up. You're killing the mood here.'

Eddy gets up from the bed and stubs out the joint.

'We need music now to lift the energy. Something contemporary or some of the old stuff?'

I feel I have lost her. She is not even talking to me. She is talking to herself. Scrolling through her playlists, looking for the song that will capture her feelings.

'How about a bit of Olivia Rodrigo? "Bad Idea Right?"'

'No. I think she's great."

Eddy is laughing. 'I wasn't asking silly. It's the name of the song. Come on dance with me.'

She has already started without me, twirling around the room, waving her arms and singing along.

23 December
The Lodge

This beautiful house is beginning to feel like a safe place in my alternative existence. Although this time, it is very different from all the other times I have visited. The house is glitzed for Christmas. An eight-foot Christmas tree stands guard by the front door. A large silver bowl containing punch is sitting on a table surrounded by crystal glasses. And a waiter is serving canapés of duck and prawn.

Eddy's mother and father are moving effortlessly through their guests. They are so unlike my parents. They have money written all over them. My parents aren't poor, but we are not rich like this. Mum has one diamond ring and a wedding band, but Eddy's mother has a handful of sparklers.

The first time I saw her was only a two-minute introduction. But now I find myself looking at her through a different lens. She is no longer Tadhg's mother, who might want to press charges for my attack on her son – she is just Eddy's mother. And she is an older version of Eddy. They have the same mischievous eyes and wide smile. She is beautiful.

I watch her being the hostess, welcoming guests, laughing at their jokes, and draping a hand over her husband's shoulder, claiming him as her own.

Suddenly I feel sad. I can imagine Eddy maturing into this world. But it is not a world I can see myself inhabiting. I won't fit into such a perfect place.

'Ros, come and meet Florrie.'

Eddy drags me towards an older woman sitting in a plush armchair, drinking sherry.

'Granny, this is a new friend of mine, Ros.'

Her grandmother eyes me almost suspiciously. 'A friend you say, or more than a friend?'

'Granny, don't be so bold. Ros is just a friend.'

There is a snort of derision from her grandmother. 'Not like that Maisie one then?'

Eddy looks caught off guard. 'No, Granny, you're such a rip. Maisie's a friend too.'

Florrie eyes me up, almost suspiciously. 'You're not a lesbian, then?'

'Granny, you can't ask my friends such things!'

'Tosh, of course I can. When you're my age you can get away with anything.' Eddy's grandmother winks at me and pats my hand. 'Doesn't matter whether you are or not, I suppose. But watch this one. She likes to flirt.'

I can tell Eddy is losing patience with her grandmother. Her usual smile disappears. She pulls me away to the kitchen.

'Sorry about Florrie. She's a head-wreck sometimes.'

'I didn't mind her. She was quite funny.'

'Would you like a drink, Ros? We even have rum and Coke tonight.'

I look at Eddy, bemused. 'Why would I want a rum and Coke?'

Eddy nudges me in the ribs. 'Don't be so rude. It's what you asked for at the first party I took you to in Rathmines, or have you forgotten?'

I laugh. 'God, I was so bloody intimidated that first night, I just asked for the first drink that came into my head. I was trying to sound sophisticated. I've never had one. My mum drinks it.'

Eddy is shaking her head at me. 'Are you serious? And I asked Tom to make sure we had rum tonight just for you. Wait until I tell him.'

'You wouldn't?'

But Eddy is now walking purposefully towards her father.

'Hey, Tom, I'd like you to meet Ros.'

Her father turns around to greet me. He is a good-looking man with a strong chin and a tanned face, but there are wrinkles around his eyes. 'Hello, Ros. Welcome to our little party.'

'Thank you for having me.'

'Oh, we didn't have much choice,' he says with a smile. 'Eddy insisted she bring her new girlfriend.'

I am blushing. I can feel it, the heat is rising from my neck to my cheeks.

'Tom, don't tease Ros. She's the shy type.'

'And she's with you! Good luck to you then, Ros. Eddy is an overly romantic firebrand at the best of times.'

A very tall man has moved into our circle of conversation and is looking to speak to Eddy's dad.

'Good party, Tom. As usual.'

Eddy takes my hand and ushers me away.

'Please don't be annoyed with me, Ros.'

'What about? For telling your father about us?'

'Yes.'

'Well, I'm not happy.'

'I'm sorry, but he guessed.'

'Why the hell would anyone guess?'

'Because I keep talking about you.'

Although her answer pleases me at one level, the fact that she has told her father still upsets me.

'Please don't be angry with me. I have a present for you.'

She takes my hand and pulls me over towards the big Christmas tree. Leaning down, she picks up a small box. 'This is for you.'

Her smile is so genuine and warm that I can't stay angry with her.

'Open it now.'

'But it's not Christmas.'

'Yes, but we can't see each other after tonight. I told you I'm going away to my uncle's, in Cork. So please open it now.'

The box is wrapped in beautiful silk paper with a little bow.

Inside the box is a silver necklace. Hanging from the chain is a symbol.

'Do you know what it is?'

'I've no idea.'

'It's the triple moon symbol from Ancient Roman times. The three images of the moon represent the maiden, the mother and the crone. It's a symbol of feminine power and intuition. Isn't it beautiful? It's all about the feminine.'

She takes the chain from my hand and puts it around my neck.

'Do you like it?'

I love that she has bought me such a thoughtful present, but I don't want to be dressed in some feminine amulet.

'But this must be expensive? We said only twenty euro.'

'Oh, it was only a little bit more. It's silver, not gold. And I got it online. Say you like it?'

I lie. I can't tell her what I really feel about it. 'It's really pretty.'

She smiles and kisses my cheek. 'It is all about us,' she says. 'It celebrates the feminine and what we do together. We celebrate being women. We don't need a man to make us happy.'

I feel the urge to vomit. My fragile world of make-believe is crumbling around my shoulders, the weight of this symbolic necklace pulling me down. My throat feels like it is closing over.

'Are you OK? You're crying.'

I hadn't noticed.

'I'm just so happy to be with you, Eddy.'

'Oh, sweet thing, that's really cute. I'm happy to be with you too. Now stop the tears and show me my present.'

'It's in my backpack. But I don't know where that is. One of those butler-type people took it from me at the door.'

'Then, it will be in the cloakroom. Behind the kitchen. Come on, we'll find it together.'

Her mood is upbeat, but I feel like someone has punched me in the stomach. I am at a party with the girl I love, but her parents think we are in a gay relationship. It's not my dream. But it is hers.

9pm
New Year's Eve
The Lodge

I am back here again. But this time Eddy is not here. She is with Maisie and other college friends at another party. She did invite me in the end, but by then I had already promised Sarah I would spend New Year's Eve with her and go to Tadhg's stupid party. Not that Sarah will even notice my presence much. Ray is responsible for her and taking her home tonight. They are official now, boyfriend and girlfriend at last, and Sarah adores the attention.

The house is heaving. Tadhg has invited *everyone*.

There are no outside heaters this time, or beer kegs in the garden – everyone is inside. The music is loud and most of my class are wearing silly Christmas cracker hats, left over from last week. Tadhg is being his usual impressive self. He is showing his rugby friends how to down a yard of ale. They clap as he dribbles it all over his chin. The kitchen floor is awash with sweet-smelling beer and mushed-in tortilla chips. It is a world away from the sophisticated party on the twenty-third. I wish I was back there with Eddy, rather than watching fools trying to impress one another.

Carl Flynn is one of the admiring crew, clapping at Tadhg's beer-swilling prowess. He sees me looking disparagingly at them.

'Hi, Ros. Leave some girls for us lads tonight, will you?'

'Get lost, Carl. You wish.'

There is still the annoying slag that I'm gay. It doesn't matter how much I protest, the title sticks. They are relentless. They see it upsets me, so they continue with it. I could report most of them for bullying at this stage, but doing so would just make them worse.

I grab a cold beer from the fridge and head for a quieter space away from the kitchen.

The main sitting room is L-shaped, with large cream couches and a grand piano. Behind the piano, I can see a cello leaning against the wall.

It is a world away from my house and my life.

This room has no family photos on the wall, but there are large paintings, modern and expensive-looking. One of them is particularly strange – a whole set of human heads impaled on cocktail sticks, facing away from one another in a circle. I stand in front of it, puzzled as to what the artist is saying. Probably something profound that would totally go over my head.

'It's bizarre, isn't it?'

I almost jump with the suddenness of the voice behind me.

'We meet again.'

Paddy Fitz is in a leather jacket, not a hair out of place, stroking his beard in a gesture which appears to question the nature of the painting in front of us.

'What the hell was this guy smoking?'

I laugh at his remark.

'More weed than I can afford to buy,' I reply.

'You look great, Ros.'

His second remark is totally unexpected, so I don't even give a reply.

'You drinking beer? To be honest I hate that weak lager. Want some rum?'

'Do you have some?' I ask.

He pulls back his jacket to reveal a bottle of Bacardi.

'Stay here and I will get some glasses and ice.'

I don't know whether to disappear upstairs into Eddy's bedroom or hang around to see what rum tastes like. It would be lovely just to lie on her bed with all her things around me. We had texted earlier in the day to wish each other a Happy New Year.

I will miss you tonight, sweet thing.

Say hello to Maisie for me.

Of course. I am lending her the book you gave me for Christmas. I loved it. We will toast the magnificence of your choice of present. I really hope you liked mine. Anyway, enjoy the party and maybe I can sneak you up to my room when I get home.

Lying on her bed would bring me close to her and maybe I could just fall asleep there until she comes home. That way we could start the New Year together. But something makes me stay in the living room, standing in front of the weird disembodied heads.

It's Paddy. He fascinates me. He is one of the few people my age that doesn't seem to give a damn about what anyone thinks of him. He is always doing his own thing.

He enters the room with two glasses of ice.

'I hope you like it neat?'

I shake my head. 'I don't know. I've actually never drunk rum before.'

'Do you know you say "actually" an awful lot? By the way, did you buy that book after all, the one you were looking at in the bookshop?'

'*Actually* I did,' I reply, stressing the word for effect.

'I'm sure your mum will love it.'

'I'm sure she won't. I've actually given it to a friend.'

'There's that word again.'

He pours himself another rum.

'Drink up or the ice will melt, and I don't want to go back into that kitchen. They're playing some dumb game now with beer bottles and straws.'

'How come you're not like them?'

He looks at me with a smile. 'What – you mean piss-heads and entitled?'

'I suppose so.'

The rum is a lot better neat than I thought it would be. A warm, fuzzy feeling is relaxing my mood.

'Probably because I had to grow up quickly. My mum died when I was ten.'

'God, I'm sorry, Paddy. I had no idea.'

'Why would you? I made a decision not to tell anyone in secondary school. It was bad enough in primary when it happened. Everyone looking at me with sad eyes and feeling sorry for me. It was my father who suffered the worst. Mum meant everything to him. They had met as teenagers and married young. He went into himself afterwards. Just worked all the time. Never home. So, I don't really know him any more, except what everyone else sees on the news.'

He is matter-of-fact about his story. He doesn't seem to be looking for sympathy.

'You really aren't like most guys, are you?'

He sits down on the couch and pats the seat beside him. 'Why?' he asks, pouring himself another rum and offering me one.

'You talk about things, emotional things.'

He pushes a strand of hair from his face and starts poking fun at me. 'Oh, wow, you really are gender heteronormative, aren't you? Stuck in old stereotypes. Expecting all us boys to behave like jocks. You're no cheerleader either.'

This time his teasing hurts me. And I can't hide it from my face or my tone. 'Because I'd bloody prefer playing sport,' I say, 'to jumping up and down on the side of the pitch.'

He laughs. 'Well, stop thinking all us guys are scared to show our emotions then.'

'Fair enough.'

It's weird to be sitting on a couch talking to Paddy Fitzpatrick. He is the poster boy in our school for the rebellious. Boys aspire to be him, and girls aspire to be with him. And I am sitting here beside him drinking rum.

My head is starting to swim. And I can hear music. It sounds like Professor Green, the rapper. It's booming through the walls.

'Do you like Green?' I ask trying to change the subject away from gender stereotypes.

'Not particularly, except one song.'

'Which one?'

'"Read All About It".'

Paddy starts smacking his leg with his hand in a clear rhythm. When he starts singing along his voice is as good as Eddy's.

'You've a good voice.'

Paddy laughs. 'Not really. But I like singing. Professor Green's father died when they were estranged. So he wrote this song.'

'Does it mean something to you, then?'

'Well, my dad might as well have died with my mum.'

Paddy stands up from the couch and starts dancing to the next track that is coming through the walls.

'This is better,' he says. 'You have to love dance music.'

I'm not a dancer but alcohol alleviates my fears of looking stupid. Unlike Paddy, I usually care about what people think of me. But not tonight. It's like a valve has blown in my head. A valve that started to blow when I found out that Eddy's father knew about us. And, tonight, the pressure is releasing, in a whirlwind of music and alcohol. I eagerly jump off the couch and start moving to the lyrics we are now shouting.

I can feel the smile on my face, and I can see Paddy smiling at me. The song is wonderfully repetitive and when it ends another one follows and another one. Wet with perspiration, we are tiring fast.

I fall to the floor and feel the spinning room has now gone into orbit. I can hear Paddy's voice, but I have no idea what he is saying. There is just his face and his breath close to mine. And I can feel an arm around my shoulder.

The world is now upside down and I am kissing someone.

Not long, slow, gentle kisses but hungry, throat exploring kisses.

I don't even notice the door to the hallway opening and people entering the room. I am kissing someone with tears in my eyes, hoping that the world will right itself soon and everything will go back into its box.

When the music stops and the house goes quiet, there's only me and Paddy in the room. We are on the couch. My head is against his shoulder, and he is asleep. I want to move, but my head is aching. I am already suffering from a massive hangover.

11.45am
New Year's Day
The Lodge

My bed is warm and comfy, but my head is screaming at me. How did I get home and what happened last night? I still feel drunk and my breath stinks of alcohol.

I pull the duvet tighter to my chin and try to snuggle back into the bed. But I need water. My throat is parched. I open one eye tentatively and a dark eye looks back at me. The eye is framed with a thick black eyebrow. It belongs to Frida Kahlo.

Shit, I'm not at home.

I scan the rest of the bedroom. I can see clothes and books that belong to Eddy. My anxiety hits the roof and rebounds back to smack me in the face.

I have snapshots of last night, snapshots that are slowly forming a film. The living room with the grand piano, Paddy Fitz and the bottle of rum, dancing on the Persian rug, falling to the floor.

Is that all there is? Why can't I remember how I ended up in Eddy's bed? And where is she?

The bedroom door opens, and Eddy stands with her hands on her hips looking at me. 'Well, you enjoyed the party last night, sweet thing.'

My throat is too dry to reply, so I let out a small groan and close my eyes.

'Don't go back to sleep. It's New Year's Day and I think you and I have some resolutions to make. Especially ones relating to alcohol. Will I get you some pain killers and a glass of water?'

I nod and feel grateful that she is leaving the room. The quietness is preferable to her voice, which although usually melodic, sounds like nails on a blackboard. If I close my eyes and go into the darkness, maybe I can develop more images of last night. The details slowly appear.

I am kissing. It's an enjoyable experience. There is a passion to it that is different from any I have felt before. It's raw and earthy.

But when I look deeper into the image I can also see that it's carnal. I am not so much kissing as devouring. My body shudders. I have never been with anyone like this before. Not even Eddy.

Did she come home when I was drunk, and did I show my sexually aggressive side to her? Suddenly the face I am kissing emerges from the darkness in my head. Jesus, that's not what happened. The face isn't Eddy's. It's Paddy Fitzpatrick.

With barely enough time to lean over the side of the bed, I vomit.

Eddy arrives back just in time to see me ruin her bedside rug.

'Oh my god, Ros, you're really in a bad way. How much did you drink last night?'

But I'm babbling now, the same words, over and over again.

'I'm sorry, Eddy. I'm sorry, Eddy. I'm really sorry.'

She is calmly removing the bedside rug. 'It's OK, Ros, don't worry. It's just an old rug, easily replaced. I don't even need a rug beside my bed.'

'No, not the rug, Ros. That's not what I mean. Not the rug.'

She sits beside me and starts stroking my forehead. 'Don't worry, sweet thing. I've been worse than this to be honest. But you really did an Oscar Wilde last night.'

I look at her confused.

'"So let's knock a couple back and make some noise." It's one of my favourite quotes of his. And, boy, were you making some noise last night when I got home. You were dancing around like a loon and singing at the top of your lungs with some good-looking guy with facial hair. To be honest, if I didn't know better, I'd think you fancied him.'

'You saw me dancing?'

'Like a loon.'

Seeing her smile at me takes my anxiety down slightly.

'I was looking for you to sneak you up to my bedroom, but when I saw you singing your little heart out, I decided you were happy where you were and left you to it.'

I don't know what to say.

Did I dream of kissing Paddy, or did it happen? Did Eddy see me kiss him or did she go to bed before I cheated on her?

So many questions need answering, but my mind can't process thoughts in an orderly fashion. It is jumping around like the rabbit from *Winnie the Pooh*, hopping from one thought to the next with alarming speed.

Eddy is still stroking my head. 'You should sleep, Ros, you look so out of it.'

But another thought has sprung into my head. Tadhg. 'Does Tadhg know I'm here in your bed?'

Eddy puts a hand gently on my arm. 'It's OK, sweet thing. He won't tell a soul.'

I am trying to sit up now, but my head is pounding. 'What do you mean, he won't tell a soul? About what?'

Eddy moves from the bed, as if to be out of reach. 'Look, you were out of your face last night. The party was over, and you were asleep on the couch in the living room.'

'On my own?'

She looks puzzled at this question. 'Yes. On your own.'

That's the answer then. I dreamt I had kissed Paddy for some ridiculous reason. Maybe it was because in my confused, drunken mind, I wanted to be safe from the destruction of my life as Rosalyn Hughes. Being with Eddy was wonderful but it was also chaotic. It stretched my boundaries to their limit.

But my mind is jumping around again. I need to stay focused.

'Eddy, what exactly did you mean when you said Tadhg wouldn't tell a soul?'

'Tadhg and I were helping mum and dad clean up after the party and we found you in the living room.'

'So?'

'So, we woke you up. Well, I woke you up and you just grabbed my arm and told me you were really sorry, and it wouldn't happen again, and you really loved me.'

I want to vomit again but there is nothing left to vomit.

I want to close my eyes and wake up in a different conversation, one where I have gone home last night with Sarah and Ray, without having drunk rum at all.

'Jesus.' It's all I can say.

I am in freefall.

I will be the laughing stock of my class.

There is no way Tadhg is not going to let this nugget loose in school.

'Ros, are you OK?' But Eddy doesn't wait for a reply. 'This is not a problem, Ros. I made him sit down with Deborah and me and we talked it out. He swore he wouldn't say anything in school. He knows Deborah and Tom are totally behind my sexuality and they won't accept any teasing or bullying. They have already experienced the pain bullying caused me in the past.'

Her words are like bleeps of a sonar. There is an echo of life outside of my head but nothing discernible. I am in the depths of dark waters. Every fear I have held of being discovered is now thriving, flourishing and growing, like some huge fungus.

'Ros, it really is all right. At some stage, people are going to know that you're gay and this is only my brother and family. No-one else will know if that's what you want. But to be honest, if you grab hold of me in front of Tadhg and tell me you love me, it's a bit of a revelation that can't be ignored. And I told you before that he overheard a conversation and was pretty suspicious anyway. Your declaration of love last night just confirmed it.'

I close my eyes.

I don't know what to say in reply.

If I close my eyes and go further into the darkness, I can hopefully hide from everything.

Eddy leans over and kisses my forehead. 'When you're feeling better, just take a shower. I will leave you a towel on the chair and some fresh clothes. But maybe sleep for now, as you do look wretched, sweet thing.'

I hear her leave the room. I think I will just escape quietly out of her bedroom and out of her life. Maybe out of all life.

But, for now, I need to sleep.

Death can wait.

6.30pm
New Year's Day
The Lodge

I can hear music. It is rising from a room below the bedroom.

It's not Eddy's music. It's classical – violins and piano, soft percussion and woodwind. It is the type of music my grandmother loves. The type that fills the house in Sandy-cove, and drifts out across the waves into the sea air.

My headache seems to have gone, replaced by a gnawing hunger. Eddy has left a pair of sweatpants and a jumper on the chair.

The shower is beautiful and reviving. It is pleasingly more powerful than the trickle in our bathroom at home. The power of the water washes a huge amount of fear from my system and takes me into another world. A world of an alternative existence. A surreal world. I have announced my love in front of her brother. I have labelled myself as gay in their eyes. And in the process given myself another mislabelled existence. I have failed to be me, the real me, yet again. Oh god!

There is just enough battery on my phone to message Eddy.

> Where are you? I'm
> showered and dressed.

The soft ping of the phone brings me a quick reply.

> Evening, sleepy head. We thought you were dead up there. I didn't want to wake you. Come down and join us.

> But I need to go home. My parents will be worried.

With all the other fears floating around my head, I had forgotten totally about my parents' response to last night.

> No. it's fine. Deborah rang your mum last night and said you were staying over.

> What did Mum say?

> I don't know.

I can imagine what my mum thought about a late-night phone call and that piece of information. But then she would have been awake anyway. The party at the golf club on New Year's Eve always runs very late.

My phone pings again.

> You haven't eaten all day.
> You should stay for dinner.
> Look, it's silly us texting. I'll
> come up.

She smiles broadly as she enters the bedroom.

'I love you being in my bed, Ros, even if you are getting over a hangover.'

I smile back. Although my smile is difficult to produce as my face feels numb.

'I'm really sorry I puked over your rug.'

'I didn't like it anyway. Mum brought it back from Morocco and I always felt it stank of camels and spices.'

'God, I feel worse now if it was a holiday gift.'

'Some holiday gifts should stay where they were bought. It didn't suit my room.'

She draws me into her arms and holds me close. 'Did you brush your teeth? I left you a new toothbrush.'

'I was hoping that was for me. Thanks.'

'Good. There is nothing worse than kissing someone who smells of stale vomit.'

When she kisses me, I feel my stomach somersault. There is a comparison happening. There is a memory resurfacing from the depths of my fuzzy head. Her kiss is passionate, but her lips are soft. There is no bristle, no scratching of my skin.

I can feel a runaway tear moving down my cheek.

'Hey, sweet thing, are you crying?'

She has stopped kissing me and is gently brushing my tears away.

'Sorry, I am all over the place. I suppose I'm still scared about Tadhg knowing. I feel unearthed.'

I'm lying yet again. I usually don't lie to Eddy. Yes, there are things I don't tell her, but I usually don't lie, and now it feels like I'm a liar. A dirty rotten liar. I can feel the need to scratch my scarred arm.

'Look, let's go down and have something to eat. Deborah has ordered pizza.'

'I don't know. I don't think I can face any of them.'

'Don't be daft, Ros, you haven't done anything wrong. You have to stop looking at lesbianism as something to apologise for. My parents are really cool with this.'

I look more than doubtful.

'Come on, Ros.' She pulls me towards her bedroom door. 'This will be good for us both. We won't have to sneak off to Rathmines. We can be here on a Saturday night and watch movies, listen to music, be open. It's a new year. Time to live a new life.'

Dinner is in the kitchen at the long oak table. Deborah, Tom and Tadhg are already seated, and I feel like I have entered the Last Supper as Judas, the betrayer. God, I wish Mr Cunningham and his religion class would get out from my head sometimes. He has no idea how some of his lessons affect me.

Eddy's parents rise to greet me, and Tadhg smiles and nods my way, but I see a look in his eye that says he is not completely behind this happy family event.

'Feeling better, Ros?' Deborah asks.

'Yes, thank you. I'm very sorry I got so drunk last night. It's not like me at all.'

A muffled 'Yeah, right' comes from Tadhg.

Eddy comes to my rescue. 'Yes. I can vouch for that. Ros is never a big drinker. I blame Tadhg.'

'Nothing to do with me,' he says. 'She was hanging around with Paddy last night. He's a drinker.'

I look at Tadhg to see if his words hold any other meaning. Does he know what I did with Paddy? But do I even know what I did with Paddy?

'Well I'm glad you're joining us for pizza, Ros,' Tom says, holding out a hand. 'Happy New Year to you.'

I sit down beside Eddy, and her mother holds out a plate of pepperoni pizza.

'Would you like some of this one, Ros, or are you a veggie, like Eddy?'

'No, pepperoni is lovely, thanks.'

'I have a Margherita for you, Eddy.'

Eddy smiles at her mum.

They are book ends to life. Eddy captures the youth and her mother the beauty of the same face, with years of experience behind it. For Eddy, it must be like looking into an ageing mirror which shows your future.

I hate mirrors. When I look into a mirror or catch a glimpse of my reflection in a window, I shudder at the female looking back at me. She shatters the illusion in my head. It is only in my face that I can see the male I believe I am. In the blueness of my eyes, the shape of my nose, the strength of my jawline.

I'm full of fears about being me. I am sitting here at dinner being afraid.

Afraid of being seen as gay.

Afraid of being outed at school.

Afraid of what I might have done last night.

My mind has wandered so obscurely from the act of eating pizza that I almost choke on the crust.

'So Eddy tells us you're brilliant at sport,' Tom says. 'Something in common with Tadhg then.'

Tadhg is visibly wincing, but trying to stay polite by not saying anything.

'Well, I play some hockey and do some athletics.'

'I think you're being a tad modest,' her father continues. 'Eddy says you're a brilliant goalkeeper.'

I smile faintly.

'Good for you,' he adds. 'My sport was athletics. Was a javelin thrower myself.'

'Come on, Tom, Ros doesn't want to hear when you threw a few,' Deborah says, teasing him.

'Oh, all right then. Just trying to make conversation and make Ros feel more relaxed.'

'I don't think that's possible, Tom,' Tadhg says. 'She's puked on Eddy's floor and come out as gay all in one night.'

'Tadhg!' There's a chorus of disapproval from his parents.

'You're such a dickhead,' Eddy adds.

'Oh Edwina, don't use such foul language. Although your sister does have a point, Tadhg. That was uncalled for.'

'No, it's fine, Mrs Morrisey, I deserved it. I'm really sorry about the rug.'

'Good lord, dear, call me Deborah, and don't think a moment about that old rug. I'm sure Eddy didn't like it much anyway.'

She glances at Eddy and gives me a smile.

'Hated it,' Eddy replies.

'See, you've done Eddy a favour. And as for coming out as gay, you did nothing of the sort. The only people here last night when you declared your love for Eddy are sitting around this table.'

I can feel my face blushing and the nausea rising in my stomach.

'And we won't say anything. Right, Tadhg?'

The question is an insistence for compliance.

'Of course,' Tadhg mumbles.

'I'm sorry if dinner was embarrassing for you. But I can tell my parents like you.'

We are lying on her bed listening to one of her many playlists.

'I don't know why. I could hardly say anything. I was so embarrassed.'

Eddy is hugging me, ignoring my conversational input. She has a lost look on her face.

'What are you thinking about?' I ask.

'Listen to the music,' she replies. 'Isn't this the most beautiful song, so poetic?'

'It's the song from that old film, isn't it? It's a film my mum loves.'

But she doesn't answer. She just sings to me. She sings the whole song.

'It's from the movie *Love Actually*.'

'It's "Both Sides Now" by Joni Mitchell.'

The song is slow, and I lie there with the feeling that something has changed between us. We now have more than just a normal bond. In my mind, we have scars, wounds of self-loathing, common ground on which to base our friendship. Except I am using the wrong word in my head. It's not a friendship. It's love.

But Eddy has healed her scar, while I'm still bleeding.

Unthinkingly, I scratch my arm through the wool of her jumper. The wounds weep. I can feel the wetness on my fingertips.

'It's a strange thing, Ros, but I have become so close to you over the last three months. I can't believe we have only known each other since October. And there is no difference in age between us. Our souls are of the same age.'

'You sound like Mr Cunningham.'

'Does he teach you RE too? He taught me. Nice man. Some odd views. But an empathetic person.'

'He's OK.'

'Do you believe in soul mates?'

I shake my head. 'I don't know whether I even believe in souls.'

'Oh, you must believe you have a soul, sweet thing. Every piece of poetry or music or heartfelt book comes from the soul. If we have no soul, then we can't truly love. The head is just a machine, a computer that processes facts, and the heart is just the organ that pumps blood around the body. But the soul, the soul is the observer of life, the lover of life, the inventor and creator. Our soul reaches out in love.'

'You really are an English student, aren't you? Everything is romantic, mushy and emotional.'

'But what else is there to life, sweet thing? Not that I agree for a moment that literature is all "mushy" as you say.'

I wish she'd stop talking. I don't want her to tell me how much she likes me or knows me or how much her soul loves me. I feel an unbearable guilt.

'Are you still feeling hungover? You're so quiet tonight.'

'That's because I should be getting home. My parents will think I've run off. They're already accusing me of strange behaviour lately, between school things and everything.'

'I don't really want to let you go. I could keep you here indefinitely as my prisoner.'

She is laughing now but I don't feel like joining in.

'Oh, come on, Ros, it's a joke. Don't be so serious all the time.'

I feign a smile and kiss her on the cheek. 'I really do need to go home.'

'OK, I'll drive you. But let's meet tomorrow. We can go for a drive, just the two of us. Maybe even take a picnic.'

'But it's January.'

'So, we can take warm clothes or eat in the car. Let's go!'

10.30pm
New Year's Day
27 Beechfield Drive

I take out a new copybook from a pile on my shelf.

Every New Year I start a new journal. I've been doing this for the last five years, starting with my aborted first year of secondary school. My counsellor at the time recommended it. 'Sometimes Rosalyn, it is good to commit your feelings to paper.'

I was unsure at first. And I was also very poor at it. I didn't understand the difference between facts and feelings. My feelings were so rarely let out of the box that I only knew how to keep my life to the construction of facts.

I am strong.

I am a good hockey player.

I am healthy.

The counsellor found it difficult to make me understand that these weren't my feelings.

'What are you feeling, Ros? Feelings are different from thoughts.'

'I am wondering whether I have missed the bus home as I want to go home.'

She would shake her head and smile at me. 'That's not a feeling, is it? That's thinking again.'

And I would get angry because I didn't see what she meant. I did want to go home, and to me that seemed like a feeling, not a thought. And anyway, what self-respecting twelve-year-old wants to sit in front of a shrink and tell them why they refuse to go to school? Because that's what happened – I had school refusal.

My parents and the school wanted to know why it was happening. My mother was particularly lost over my refusal to attend, as if I had let her down as the only other female in the family. Ian was a good boy, like his dad, but I was a reluctant teenager. Had she affected me in some way to make me upset and anxious? Had she failed in her mothering?

'First year is full of new experiences and daunting changes from primary school but most children find their way through it, Rosalyn. Why can't you try?'

But I knew I wasn't like most children. Most children are boys or girls, and I was some strange hybrid – a boy in a girl's body. And I had coped with this existence until puberty started. But then puberty forced me further into the world of a female.

'So why won't you go to school, Rosalyn? What scares you about it?'

I couldn't tell either the counsellor or my mum that it wasn't school that scared me but interacting with people. My chest had grown into a shape that I loathed, my hips had started to broaden, and my body had started to bleed on a regular basis. I knew everyone else in my class would see the same girl on the outside that I hated. There would be no ambiguity about my gender any longer. I screamed female through every pore.

Before puberty I had looked more androgynous. Now I stank of female.

The counsellor tried for six months to make me talk about my feelings. And my parents drove me to school every Monday. But my walls didn't come down. I was glued to my bed and my Xbox and any other screen that could give me an alternative world in which to live.

Before puberty, I had imagined that my voice would deepen, and hair would grow on my chest. I was so convinced of my maleness that I believed that puberty would come to my rescue and show the world the real me. But it did the opposite. It shattered my inner reality. Flung me into a world of femininity that I couldn't deal with. In fact, I just refused.

By the time I was thirteen, I had reconciled myself to the monthly periods and growing breasts. I hated them, but I couldn't see a way of removing them. So, I reluctantly decided to go to school and avoid any conversation about them or me. I would talk about sports, films, video games and food but never about what made me tick. I became an emotional recluse.

I take the pen from my bedside locker now.

A new journal. I have to make the first few words count. I don't want them to be boring or badly written. But I can't put a word on the blank page. Instead, my pen starts doodling. Loads of little boxes. And disconnected pipes. I am getting angrier as they sprout all over the page. Then random letters start to appear. Capital letters. E, A, R, S.

What am I doing?

I look at the letters again. It's not 'ears' but 'arse'! I have spelt 'arse' over and over again in big, black, bold capital letters.

That's me. I am an arse. I have the most beautiful girl wanting to be my girlfriend and I am kissing another person. Because I know I have kissed Paddy. The details of last night have become clearer as the alcoholic haze has worn off.

What was I thinking?

Was I trying to be normal? Trying to fit my ugly body back into Pandora's box.

But if I could fall for someone like Paddy, then maybe I could exist in this body, exist as a female. Wouldn't that be easier than a life trying to explain to people why I'm male? I could maybe have a normal life, get a job, get married, live in a house like No.27.

Bile reaches the back of my throat and I swallow it down.

Jesus, no. That's not the answer. Imagine being a wife, being pregnant, giving birth – the horror of it makes my doodles even angrier.

But why am I so scared of being with Eddy?

I start to write a string of words in my journal.

Dear me, it is a new year and I have the chance of creating a new life, but I am scared. I have hidden who I am for so long that I am scared to reveal him to the world in case he is rejected by all those I love. What if they walk away from me? What if my parents disown me? What if Sarah is disappointed in me for lying to her all these years? What if me being male makes her feel awkward about our sleepovers and hugs? What if Eddy doesn't want to be with a male but only wants to be lesbian? She could look at me and tell me it's all over and that I'm not what she wants. She wants the old Ros, not some transformed person called Adrian.

I put the pen down. God, where did that name come from? I had never thought of a name for my male self before. I had presumed I would go from Ros to Ross. But maybe that's not enough of a change. It needs to make people realise I'm a different person altogether. But Adrian isn't a good name. Sure, it's a girl's name anyway if spelled differently.

I make a list of some names that I might like for my male persona:

Zachary – very different but too American.

Howard – too old fashioned.

Stephen – no that would be weird, he's my first cousin.

Noah – I quite like that. It's short and it doesn't have a feminine form.

I draw a little image of an ark in my journal. But then the image irritates me. Noah is out of the question. He only had two of each animal in his ark – male and female. He didn't save any animals like me, a blend of both. But maybe I'm not meant to be saved, maybe I am a freak that needs to be eliminated from the planet. The Bible thumpers would like to do that – they don't see the necessity for people like me. And sometimes I don't see the need for my existence either.

Maybe that's why I hate myself so much. Because I don't fit in. I don't want to be different. I want to be part of the binary. I want to be seen and exist as male.

I scratch a scab from a cut and rub the blood into my finger. I feel I should be challenging society to see me as the person I am, and not just my outer shell.

A new word has appeared on my page.

Eddy.

I draw a box around it and put the box into a loveheart. Would she love me if she knew?

There is a soft knock on my bedroom door.

'Yeah.'

'It's only me. I was wondering if we could have a chat, Rosalyn. I haven't seen much of my beautiful daughter lately.'

My mum is standing in the doorway, holding two mugs.

'I brought you some hot chocolate. I thought we could sit on your bed and chat about the New Year's resolutions we're going to make. We used to do it when you were small, remember?'

I want to finish my journal and sleep, but she is not my usual buoyant mum this evening. She seems sad and emotional.

'Yeah, sure. That would be nice.'

I shut my journal and place it in my bedside locker.

'No, keep it out. We can make our resolutions in it.'

'It's my English copybook, Mum.'

'Oh, OK, well I'm sure we can remember them anyway.'

She sits on the edge of my bed and puts a hand on my arm. It is not the arm with the painful little cuts. I have managed to keep those hidden from my family.

'I've got one for you, Rosalyn. You could give up alcohol this year.'

'Jesus, Mum, the whole idea is for me to come up with my own resolutions, not have them enforced. I thought this was supposed to be a sharing thing and not an intervention.'

Usually, my mother would fight back and assert her viewpoint, but tonight she just sits there and apologises.

'Are you OK, Mum?'

'Oh, of course. Just tired after last night's party. Probably too much alcohol myself, so maybe I am the one who should give it up.'

She nudges me over in the bed to make room for her.

'Can I just lie beside you for a while? Remember the books I used to read to you? You loved Dr Seuss and the one about all the way to the moon and back.'

'*Guess How Much I Love You.*'

'Yes, that was it. It had a mummy and baby rabbit on the cover.'

'Yeah, I loved it. It's here in my bedroom somewhere.'

'Not in the attic with your other old stuff?'

'No, I couldn't bear to part with it. The attic seemed so cold and horrible a place to keep such a lovely book.'

My mother puts an arm around me and hugs me tightly.

'Are you sure you're OK, Mum? You haven't lain on my bed for months.'

She smiles almost distractedly. 'Oh, that can't be right, Rosalyn.'

But I nod.

'Well, I'm sorry if that's the case. Life does get very busy with the writing club and golf, yaddy ya.'

'That's such a strange expression. You use it a lot.'

'What? Yaddy ya?'

'Yes.'

'Gosh, I suppose I do. I think I got it from your granny. I do miss her since they have gone to Spain.'

The conversation is pottering along and I'm so tired and need to sleep.

'So what's your resolution, Mum?'

'To make each day count, love. We never know when it may be our last.'

'That's a bit heavy.'

She doesn't react to my statement, as she is teary-eyed.

'Mum, what is it?'

'The first of January is more than just New Year's Day – it's also the anniversary of your uncle's death, my little brother, Kenneth. It's been twenty years.'

I take her hand and squeeze it gently.

'Twenty years, Ros, and it seems like it happened yesterday. He was such a beautiful young man, you know. Looked a lot like --'

'David Bowie.'

'Yes, David Bowie, without the pink hair and make-up.'

She has stopped crying, but she is still in a world remote from her usual self.

'He was a clever boy. He devoured books, mostly the classics. He had so much going for him, but he was just too sensitive for this world. Your grandma said he had a tortured soul, but we all know why he did it. There was no confusion about that. It's something your grandparents couldn't talk about. You look a lot like him, Rosalyn, but with a stronger frame and jawline.'

'He looked more feminine,' I add.

My mother turns to face me and shakes her head. 'Don't say that, Rosalyn! You're very feminine, and a good-looking girl too. But he was just so thin and almost fragile.'

With a quickness that surprises me, my mother raises herself up from my bed.

'I'm sorry, Rosalyn, I've whittered on and we haven't even talked about your resolutions. But I'm suddenly very tired. Can we do it at breakfast tomorrow?'

'Of course, Mum.'

She ruffles my hair and turns to the door.

'You can be whatever you want to be in life, Rosalyn. Your uncle was scared to be who he was, and it cost him his life.'

I don't take my journal back out of the drawer when she leaves. I have no more energy to write anything. I pull the duvet up to my chin and wonder whether I can tell Eddy the truth tomorrow.

Ding, ding.

Damn, I have forgotten to put my phone on silent. Maybe it will be Eddy saying good night.

> Hi Ros. Hope you don't
> mind me texting you so late

It's not her. I don't even recognise the number, so I type a quick reply.

> Who's this?

> God, sorry, it's Paddy

My heart sinks and my stomach twists all at the same time. Maybe I shouldn't reply. But I can't resist finding out what he wants.

Hi Paddy

I just wanted to say I really enjoyed last night. Had far more fun than I thought I would at Tadhg's.

Me too

What the hell? Am I automatically writing from my stupid side? Am I mad? Don't write that, dumbass.

Want to go to the cinema tomorrow and see that film we were talking about?

I have no idea what film. I don't remember any conversation – just drinking, dancing and sharing saliva.

Lots of tickets left so you don't have to decide now. Let me know before lunch tomorrow. Goodnight x

Night

I put my phone on silent and throw it into the bedside locker. This is not good. And what was with that little 'x' on the end of his message?

8pm
2 January
The cinema

'I wasn't too sure you'd come.' Paddy is standing in front of the cinema attendant holding out two tickets.

'Oh, I like going to films. It's escaping into another world for two hours.'

We head up the stairs towards screen one. I have given Eddy an excuse not to meet her tonight. I have a bad cold. A possible flu. I hope I haven't given it to her. We can meet next week when I'm better. She sends me heart emojis and kisses. I feel guilty. In the last three months my life has been turned on its head by the arrival of Eddy and I'm still spinning.

'How come you wanted to come here, Ros? We've cinemas much closer.'

'That's the problem. There would be people there from school and I just didn't want –'

'To be seen with a rebel, a school dropout?'

I shake my head. 'Not at all. I like the fact that you're your own person and don't take anything without question.'

Paddy has chosen seats in the middle of the large theatre.

'I'm a bit picky where I sit,' he says. 'I can't be at the front as I sat there once for a Bond film when the cinema was jam-packed. I thought I was going to throw up during the car chases. Everything was a speedy blur.'

'And what's wrong with sitting at the back?' I ask.

'People sit there not to watch the film and I didn't want you to think I'd brought you here just to make out. Besides, I'd need my glasses that far back.'

'I didn't know you wore glasses.'

'There's lots of things you don't know about me.'

'Tell me some then.'

I like hearing him talk. He is calm and mature about everything. He doesn't get angry or fazed, even though he is passionate about societal problems, problems of which I have no understanding. I feel immature in his company but also strangely safe. I feel like I have walked out of chaos and into something stable and supportive. He doesn't push me out of the boundaries of my constructed reality. He anchors me to Ros Hughes. And no matter how much I hate being her, I have lived with her for seventeen years and she is familiar to me. My grandmother has a phrase which sums it all up perfectly – better the devil you know.

Ros Hughes is the devil I know.

The male side of me wants to deconstruct my present reality and venture out into uncharted waters, but I'm not sure I have the strength of character to blaze new trails. Paddy is a safe harbour.

'I have a lizard called Lenny. A dog called Petra. And I now live in the basement of my grandmother's house in Rathmines.'

'You don't live with your dad any more?'

'No. He's got his politics and I have my own brand of anarchy.'

'Such as?'

'I have joined Friends of the Earth.'

'Why not the Green Party?'

'Huh, that's exactly what my dad said. Join a group that can at least make a change politically to support the environment. But they're tied into the system.'

I'm smiling at Paddy.

'What are you smiling at? Do I amuse you?'

'I am just thinking about how different we are. You care about the world outside of yourself and I only care about how I exist within this world.'

He leans over and offers me more popcorn. His bearded face is close to mine.

'That's very deep of you, Miss Hughes.'

The words make me wince.

'Don't call me that, please. I'm just Ros.'

He looks confused but shrugs his shoulders.

'Sorry. I'm slightly nervous today.'

'Why?'

'It's a long time since I've been on a date. In fact, it's a long time since I've asked a girl out.'

I stand up. The cinema is still showing the adverts, but most people have taken their seats.

'I'm sorry, Paddy. I can't do this. I'm sorry.'

He spills his popcorn getting up from his seat and I can hear him apologise to other people as he squeezes past them to come after me.

'Ros, wait.'

But I'm faster than him. Years of hockey training help. I am out through the cinema door before he has made it down the stairs. From behind the street corner, I watch him run into a shopping centre. He has chosen the wrong direction. I am heading out to the main road and down towards the railway station.

I'm sitting on the cold metal seats, waiting for the DART to come. My phone is pinging relentlessly.

What did I say?

Are you OK?

Can we meet for a drink?

If you don't like me, it's fine

Where are you?

God, I hate this

Ros?

I feel mean. He didn't deserve me bolting out of the cinema. He is one of the nicest people I have ever met. He is thoughtful, kind, and he likes me! But he likes a *version* of me. Just like Eddy likes a version of me. No-one likes the real me.

10.20am
Monday 8 January
English class

Now I have made one lie fit all. Both Eddy and Paddy have been given the same weak excuse. *I'm sorry, I'm still not feeling well.* Because I did eventually text Paddy back. I told him that I had suddenly felt like vomiting in the cinema, and I didn't want him to see me sick. I told him it must have been a hangover from the party two days before. He accepted my excuse.

> It's OK. We can go again.
> But you should have said.
> Petra vomits and I'm fine
> with her.

So at this moment in time, I have two people dangling off my excuse of illness, and I don't wish to see either of them again, but I also don't want to be on my own. I love Eddy, but life with her brings chaos. It brings the immediate threat of exposure and life-changing revelations. Whereas Paddy offers a respite from all that destruction. In fact, he offers an alternative. A way to stay as Ros Hughes. I know what my grandmother would say: 'You can't make an omelette without breaking eggs.' So maybe I should break from everything and make a new life as a male.

In some ways, I haven't lied to either Paddy or Eddy. I have felt sick all week. I have been unable to eat. Even my mum has commented on more than one occasion that I'm not eating enough and it's not like me.

Sitting beside Sarah in English class, I want to tell her everything and ask her to help me out of all this. But she is so happy with Ray, and so normal in every way. I can't see her understanding such an abnormal existence. She has known me for too many years. She is completely invested in my life as Ros Hughes. Ros is who she knows and loves. Telling her would be like killing off her favourite character in a soap opera.

My spiralling thoughts are disturbed by Mr Cunningham.

'Hello again, 4B. Today as we start a new term, we begin the Creative Writing module. It is where you get the chance to invent a whole new world.'

Some rip starts singing the Disney song, but Cunningham is not to be deterred. He has the same relentless approach to getting the work done that he has in Religion class.

'There are no boundaries to what you can create. Look at George Orwell's *Animal Farm*, where animals rebel against their human farmer. The anthropomorphism of that book is fascinating. Does anyone know what that word means?'

Very few heads stir from their recumbent positions, and I'm one of the many who couldn't give a damn; but Eamonn is happy to beat Jessica to the response.

'It means to give animals human characteristics, sir. Like we do with Carl here.'

Carl lobs a pencil case in Eamonn's direction, but there is no malice meant. For some reason none of us can understand, Carl likes Eamonn. They have a relationship that seems to feed on neither of them being particularly liked. But now I see Eamonn in a different light. Paddy likes him.

Cunningham chooses to ignore the interaction between Eamonn and Carl.

'So what I would like you to do,' he continues, 'is to look at society and turn some aspect of it on its head. Find a new world you can create in your essay.'

If I could create a new world, it would be a world where gender doesn't matter at all. A world where you can decide your own gender and be with anyone you wish without censure.

'OK, let's have some ideas about turning the world on its head. Just shout them out when you think of anything, and I will put them on the whiteboard.'

But it's only 10.20 in the morning and most of us are still not fully awake.

'Tadhg, what kind of world would you create in your essay?'

Tadhg hasn't really been paying attention. It's his default setting to sleep in class when not sending notes around.

'Me, sir?'

'Yes, you, Tadhg!'

'I don't know, sir, everything I'd like to write about has already been done in films or books – zombie apocalypses, alien invasions.'

Cunningham is undefeated by Tadhg's reticence about creating something new.

'So how would you make those topics fresh and interesting, Tadhg?'

Tadhg looks around his crew and grins.

'Well, sir, we could have alien abductions.'

'I think you'll find they've been done too, Morrisey,' Eamonn interrupts.

'If I can continue, gothman,' Tadhg says. 'In my essay, the only humans the aliens abduct would be teachers so that they can programme them to indoctrinate the world with alien ideas.'

Cunningham smiles. 'I can imagine you'd like to have me abducted alright, Tadhg.'

'Now did I say that, sir?'

Cunningham gives Tadhg a wry smile.

There is a murmur of surprise around the classroom that Tadhg has provided a reasonable storyline. But not everyone is impressed.

'That's not fiction,' Eamonn sneers, giving Tadhg a disparaging look. 'We are already being indoctrinated by the education system. Look at Paddy Fitzpatrick.'

Cunningham raises an eyebrow at the comment from our resident goth. 'I don't think we need to bring Paddy Fitzpatrick up in this class,' he suggests.

I am in full agreement with Mr Cunningham. I don't want to think about Paddy Fitzpatrick.

'But I think we do, sir. We are all indoctrinated here. Paddy wasn't allowed to wear earrings or have long hair due to archaic school rules. It's ridiculous. And I'm not allowed to wear my usual black eyeliner. We are being moulded into pathetic replicas of our teachers and their teachers before them. The school system is nothing more than a creation of the industrial system to provide compliant workers. We are being groomed to have no thoughts of our own and yet you ask us to be creative. Where is our creativity allowed?'

At this last dramatic statement, Eamonn stands up from his seat and turns to face the entire class. A round of applause echoes around the room.

It is something entirely unplanned but, stirred by Eamonn's rousing speech, I also begin ranting.

'And what about the gender indoctrination that goes on?'

A confused class turns towards me. But I have already fallen over the precipice and I continue falling.

'Boys can do this. Girls can do that. We are taught how to gender-behave from the moment that we can walk. We are trapped in stupid stereotypes, pink for girls and blue for boys, that leaves that lot acting like jocks and those acting like bimbos.'

I have crossed the line now and referred to both Tadhg's crew and the Flock in less than flattering ways. I plough on with my outpouring as quickly as I can, hoping to take their focus away from my insults.

'We are not supposed to leave our stupid stereotypes or behave in any way contradictory to gender norms. And yet we say we support the LGBTQ+ community, but we hardly offer any support bar a few words in wellbeing class, and some cringeworthy assemblies on Rainbow Day. Every toilet we have is still gender binary, and every gym class divided into male or female. It's pathetic. So, yes, I agree with Eamonn. We are all being indoctrinated.'

Sarah is tugging at my skirt, trying to get me to sit down. But at this stage, I have burned my bridges and tears have formed in my eyes. Without saying another word, I exit the door and escape into the corridor, shutting the door firmly behind me. Gasping for air, I head towards the locker room. I can hear the classroom door opening and Cunningham's voice call after me.

But I don't look back.

I'm leaving.

11.45am
Monday
Sandycove

Luckily, I remember the code for the alarm on the front door. Throwing my schoolbag into the hall cupboard, I walk into the large open-plan kitchen and look out at the stormy sea at the back of the house. Thank god my grandparents are still in Spain.

I can feel that my eyes are red and puffy. All the way from the DART station I have wiped the tears from my face with the sleeve of my jumper.

My mind is in freefall. The large warehouse of my subconscious, with all its carefully stored boxes, is now looking as if a bomb has hit it. Thoughts and fears are tumbling out onto the floor.

I look around the tidy kitchen and see the block of knives. They are too big, too emphatic. Opening the drawer, under the granite worktop, I find a smaller knife, with a shocking pink handle. The pinkness of it irritates me and I throw it back into the drawer and slam it shut. But I have this overwhelming ache to add to the line of scars across my arm. Opening the drawer again, I find a different knife, black-handled and sharp.

Pulling back my sleeve, I reveal all the other lines of self-hatred. If I can just peel off my skin and stop being me, then I can live a better life than this one. It is my outer shell that is the problem. My head is fine. I'm not mad or anything.

As I slump down on the tiled floor, my chest heaves with the stupidity of it all.

But I'm in love. I'm in love with a girl who loves me. Because, although it has only been three months, we had been inseparable. Until I messed it all up with Paddy.

I tug the small pendant from below my school shirt and hold it tightly in my hand. And she has even given me this stupid necklace. She believes it shows what we mean to each other. Two females together. But that's not me.

How can she fit in with my awful life? She is the one area of happiness in the darkness of my being here, and yet she doesn't know me either. She just thinks she does, or she wouldn't have given me this. I tear the pendant from my neck and throw it to the floor.

Every night we have messaged each other from under warm duvets. She sends me songs, and we listen to the lyrics and find meanings that can be applied to our relationship. But Eddy resides in a false reality. She is blissfully unaware, and I have kept her there out of fear of rejection.

I'm not female.

I'm not a girl.

And I will never become a woman.

That's what's wrong with being with Paddy too. He also wants to be with a girl, and I refuse to be one.

Jesus. Everyone wants me to be a stupid girl. But I will prevent that from happening. And I will do it in one of two ways: I will transform or I will die.

It is windy outside in the back garden. The grass is damp under my feet, and I can taste the salt on my tongue from the sea spray. Hurting my hands on the jagged stones, I climb on the back wall and stare at the rocks below. The distance is only about a metre, but I'm worried about hurting myself. If I jump, I could break an ankle. The ridiculousness of the situation makes me laugh. Two minutes ago, I was prepared to drag a sharp blade across my skin and now I'm worried about turning an ankle on slimy rocks.

My phone is ringing. It has been ringing incessantly for the last hour. I take it out of my pocket and glance at the screen. My mother again. The last three calls have all been from her. Before her, there were four calls from Sarah, and an unknown number which I presume is the school. They will be furious that I have left the premises.

Losing my fear, I jump. Luckily, I land solidly on a large rock. The sea is close now. Leaning forward, I can almost touch the water with my hand.

I have always loved water. The weightlessness of being suspended, the cocooning feeling of floating in a calm sea. But today's sea is rough. It's as angry as my mood.

A message pings. There have been countless messages too. But these latest ones are all from Sarah.

> Ros, your mum and dad
> have been told

> We couldn't find you in school, so the office rang home looking for you

> Are you OK?

> What happened today? Is it what we were talking about recently?

My fingers hesitate above the letters. I want to write back. I want to tell my best friend that she doesn't have a clue who I am. I want to shock her with the truth.

But I can't.

They can read it in my journal when I'm gone. It's all there in blue biro, in the hardback notebook I keep in the drawer of my desk at Beechfield Drive. I can imagine my mother finding it first. Sitting on my bed, the notebook in her hands, tears running down her face. She would see how much I hate being a girl, how I bandaged my chest when I was younger. How I cried for weeks when the periods started, when the cutting began.

I feel sorry for her, sitting there wondering how she failed me. But there is no failure on her part. I'm just a fluke of nature, an abnormality. I must be abnormal, as everywhere around me there are girls happy to be girls, and boys happy to be boys. It is only me who looks at my body as if it is the product of an alien abduction. I scratch at my arm and open the wounds. The pain is something I welcome, as if hurting my arm is damaging the body that causes all my problems.

I should have been born a boy. Puberty should have given me a deeper voice and a small bit of stubble, not wider hips and stupid breasts. The binding of course didn't work so I started hunching over to avoid showing. My mother would give out to me for walking like Quasimodo. 'Stand up straight, Rosalyn,' she would say. 'Why do you insist on walking that way?'

Because I hate myself, mother. And I hate these breasts. And it has been my bloody luck to grow breasts bigger than most girls in my year. What the hell is that all about? A punishment for thinking I'm male. My karma for not accepting my femininity!

The sea is coming closer to me. I feel drawn to let go of my refuge on the rock. But that would be a disaster. I don't want my mother reading my journal. She would stand at my funeral, glaring at poor Eddy as she cries over my coffin. Eddy is in my journal in descriptive passages. The nights we have spent together. The things we have done. It is all in the pages of my journal. And I don't want anyone to think I'm gay. And that could be the conclusion they come to. I have never used the word 'transgender' in my journal. Self-hatred is all that comes across when you look through the pages.

Hopefully my mother is too busy looking for me to search through my desk. I suddenly start feeling the cold. The sea spray has soaked through to my underwear. I shiver and step back from the edge. I can't do it. I can't end my life. I do have Eddy. I can remove all signs of Paddy from my phone and go back to being with her. Maybe I can contain the chaos.

Maybe if I tell her about me, then we can have a relationship built on more than a lie. She can be at my side when I go for surgery. She can help me take the medication and deal with any side effects that happen. Eddy would do that. She is kind, thoughtful and loving.

I climb back over the wall and head into the warmth of the house.

The coffee heats me from the inside. Sitting on my grandparents' couch, I can see the photos of our family on the mantelpiece. I try looking at myself with the eyes of a stranger. My thick brown hair is short and what my mother would refer to as 'tidy'. In reality, I am not a very pretty girl, despite what my mother says. Not the type that teenage boys find attractive. The sound of Eddy's voice echoes through my thoughts. The lyrics of the song she sang to me. 'Love is meant for beauty queens'. And I am an ugly duckling.

Though Paddy would disagree with me. He thinks I'm worth a date to the cinema.

I feel sad that I was not born perfect. I feel sad that I can't go back to the cinema with him and just enjoy being a girl. How easy would that be, to live a life that conforms?

The face in the photo on the mantelpiece screams back at me: 'I'm not female, I'm male!' But all I can see is a misfit who is trying to persuade the world of something that is not obvious at all.

The phone pings again. It's Eddy. I can feel the smile on my face. I need her warmth and love now.

> Hi there, sweet thing. I've missed you this week. So glad you're feeling well enough to go to school. What are you doing now? I've been rereading your present. That woman is inspiring. I feel like running away to have adventures.

I hesitate with my reply, trying to think of a reason for my visit to my grandparents' house. But my phone impatiently pings again.

> Hello??

I pause over what to write. Eventually I move my fingers across the screen.

Hi. I'm at my grandparents, watering their plants. They're away. Want to come visit?

I thought you were in school

Free afternoon. Rugby match.

OK. So where do they live?

Sandycove

There is a pause while she is presumably thinking whether she wants to make the journey.

It's not far from the DART, Eddy.

I hope this fact will attract her.

No, I have my car today. I'll be out in an hour. Send me the address.

I send her the address and decide to turn off my phone. I suspect that since my parents know about my school absence, they may go to the police and phone tracking will be used. Or maybe I am just going into the realms of fantasy. They are both working today. Mum does charity work every Thursday and wouldn't have time to worry about my whereabouts. The Ros she knows is dependable and organised, not chaotic and disobedient. She will assume that I will return home for dinner when I'm hungry and have a good reason for my disappearance. She trusts me. I have never given her cause to panic, except for that pen-throwing incident. The school refusal thing was years ago; she's got over that. And as for my father, he ignores all school issues and presumes my mother will deal with them. He is not a modern-day type of father. Parenting is for the wife.

'It's freezing out there. And not easy to find a parking space around here. Do you know there are some really dumb human beings swimming off the harbour in this weather?'

Eddy is standing at the door, looking decidedly wet. 'As you can see, I had to park ages away,' Eddy says, shaking rain from her hair.

'I'm sorry,' I say. 'It wasn't raining when I invited you. Come in and I will make you coffee.'

'No worries. Two sugars. I don't suppose you have vegan-friendly milk?'

'Not even vegan-unfriendly milk. I was only coming here to water the plants.'

'It doesn't matter.' Eddy looks around the house. 'Lovely place they have. This belong to your dad's parents?'

'No, my mum's.'

Admiringly, she walks through the front rooms and into the back kitchen.

'Wow, that's a beautiful view. Private access to the sea. Fantastic. I wish my parents had a romantic house like this rather than that oversized show of wealth.'

'But your parents' house is gorgeous.'

'Oh, sweet thing, it's ostentatious. Whereas this house is where Yeats or Wilde could have lived. It has that vibe of authenticity about it.'

I laugh. 'We really don't have much in common, do we, Eddy? I'd far prefer to live in your warm, huge home rather than this draughty relic of a house.'

'But look at that view. Those waves are practically lashing over the wall into the garden.'

'The view is even better from upstairs.'

Eddy gives me a glance of mock disapproval. 'Are you trying to lure me upstairs?'

'Maybe.'

'Whose room is this?'

I roll over on the bed and look out of the window. The rain has stopped.

'It's just a guest room, but it was my uncle's when he lived here.'

Eddy pulls on her T-shirt and walks over to the bookcase. 'Are these his? He has good taste.'

I can't concentrate on her question, as she is standing with her back to me, and I can see her nakedness below the T-shirt.

'Look at all these – Whitman, Woolf, García Lorca, Truman Capote. He has so many wonderful books.'

She picks up a small pink book and blows the dust off the cover.

'Then there's this strange little gem amongst the others. It's a first edition. What a wonderful little book to own! Why does he leave them all here?'

It is not a question I want to answer, but I am unable to refuse Eddy anything.

'He's dead.'

Eddy places the book down and turns to face me.

'God, I'm sorry, Ros. Was it recent?'

'No, he died before I was born. I never knew him.'

'How sad. What happened to him?'

I sit up and wonder whether I should tell his story. My grandparents hardly mention him. I decide it can't hurt to tell his truth.

'Is this him?' Eddy has a photo frame in her hand. 'You look a bit like him, Ros. He has the same sad eyes and beautiful cheek bones. He's very good-looking, almost like a young David Bowie. How did he die?'

I take the photo from her and look at the face of my uncle. He is a stranger to me although I am his blood relative.

'He died by suicide. My family obviously doesn't talk about it much. Except my mum did recently as it was twenty years ago on New Year's Day.'

Eddy looks shocked. 'I'm so sorry. I shouldn't have asked. I just wanted to know about the man who owns these books.'

'I don't know much about him at all, except that his nickname was Tigger, and he was supposedly great fun until something happened to him in his late teens. Nobody talks about it really.'

Eddy picks up the small hard-back book again.

'Maybe that's why he owned this,' she suggests. *The House at Pooh Corner.* I love AA Milne.'

I pat the bed beside me. 'Come back. It's cold.'

Eddy walks to the bed and lies down beside me. She is still holding the small book in her hand.

'If you were a character from *Winnie the Pooh*, who would you be, sweet thing?'

'God, I don't know. I suppose I'm a bit of a Rabbit.'

She laughs at me and nods. 'Yes, I can see that – always running around and having to do something. Always active. Almost afraid to sit still.'

I poke her gently in the ribs. 'Hey, that's not fair. I'm sitting still now.'

'Only because you wanted to do something. Of which I'm very glad. I did miss you this week.'

She opens the book and turns the pages, looking through the images of the well-known characters.

'Who do you think I'm most like, Ros?'

I rub my chin, pretending to put effort into my reply. 'Owl, that's blatantly obvious.'

'Oh no! Do you see me as a know-it-all, just fluttering around delivering facts to the world?'

'OK, don't get upset. You're not just Owl. You're also motherly like the kangaroo.'

'Like Kanga?'

'Yes, like Kanga. And I suppose you're fun and bubbly like Tigger.'

'OK, that's better. And you're also like Winnie the Pooh because you're very fond of your food,' she adds.

I'm relieved that we have moved past the sadness that Uncle Kenneth had brought into the room, but she is still lost in his story.

'Did he die in this room?'

'God, Eddie, that's a dark question to ask.'

'I'm sorry. It's just that I have a strange feeling that someone has been watching us since we've come here.'

'Don't say that. There's no such thing as ghosts. And I'd hate to think of him watching us. Anyway, he didn't die in this room.'

I stand up and pull her from the bed towards the window.

'Do you see out there, the small pile of stones at the edge of the sea?'

'What, the little man-made mound in a cone shape?'

I nod.

'That's where he died. He drowned off the rocks there. He threw himself into the sea.'

'Oh, the poor man! How much pain must he have been going through to do that? So many wonderful writers have died by suicide, you know – Ernest Hemingway, Virginia Woolf, Sylvia Plath. It seems to be the path of the tortured artistic soul.'

I'm crying now. I can't stop the tears. They are rolling softly down my cheek.

'God, Ros, I'm so very sorry. I shouldn't have brought all this up. I'm sorry. He was your uncle. I should have kept quiet.'

'I'm not crying for him, Eddy. I told you I didn't know him. It's you and me. We've hurt ourselves out of pain too. And I've thought of ending my life.'

She turns to face me and takes my hand in hers. 'That's all in the past, sweet thing. We're fine now. We have each other and we have the support we need for who we are.'

She hugs me tight, and I can feel her breath on my neck. I feel a sense of belonging that I've never felt before. The events at school have no part in this relationship. They are another world away, a different dimension. They are not here in this bedroom, with the sea crashing on the shore and the wind rattling the window frames. The ugliness of school can't affect this beauty. I have done what Mr Cunningham has asked: I have created a whole new world.

I realise that I am becoming Eddy, becoming romantic and emotional.

'I'm so glad you came here today, Eddy.'

'Me too. I feel I know you even more now, seeing where your grandparents live. And being in a bed associated with you, rather than at my friends or my home.'

'Does it matter?' I ask.

'Of course it does, silly. You're welcoming me into your world. You haven't told your family about us yet, so I've never seen inside your house. But in this small way I have become a part of your world by sleeping here with you. It's nice being in your world for a change.'

An anxious thought crosses my mind.

'But I hate that your brother knows about us, Eddy. I could hardly look at him in school today.'

She wraps her arm around me, but it doesn't fill me with confidence.

'Look, he won't say anything, Ros. He knows better than to upset my parents about something like this. Anyway, he didn't say anything to you in school this morning, did he?'

'No. He said nothing.'

'Well then, it's all OK. Just forget about him.'

But a crack has appeared in the wall that keeps our relationship safe. I feel I am floating out the window and sinking into the sea. The dark water around me is filling my airways and I can't breathe. The more I think about school and my outburst in the classroom, the more my head hurts.

'Eddy, I hate people thinking they know me!'

'Honestly, Ros, there's nothing to worry about.'

'But you've no idea what I've done. Today in school, I was a complete lunatic in front of the class.'

'What do you mean?'

'I babbled on about gender stereotyping and the indoctrination of children into binary norms. I completely unravelled. And that's what's happening to me, Eddy. I'm unravelling.'

Eddy hugs me closer. 'You don't need to panic, Ros. People are going to find out you're gay one day and it will be OK in the end if you just don't react to any teasing that happens.'

'God, you're the one who told me not to come out too quickly, as you were bullied in school.'

'Yes, but I was much younger than you. You're seventeen and a stronger person than I was.'

I get up from the bed and start dressing.

'I need to go home, Eddy.'

'Come on, Ros, I'm sorry. I don't know what to say to you. It's OK to be seen for who you are. There's no need to be afraid. Look at my life. I have friends who know me and love me, and you will be the same. And we have each other.'

But I can't talk to her any more. My head is swimming in circles.

'It's time we left, Eddy. I have to be home for dinner.'

5.15pm
Thursday
The DART

As I sit on the packed train, I can feel my fingernails digging into the flesh of my palms. I am cold and tired. There is a slowness to the moving train that irritates me. I don't want to sit surrounded by people I don't know, jostling for leg space as their knees bang into mine.

Eddy left me at the station. She kissed me as I got out of the car and she headed off to see a friend. I watched her car disappear down the road and thought of going back to my grandparents' house. I had no desire to face my parents or anyone else, especially my class and Mr Cunningham. But I'm hungry and my grandparents' house is cold and empty without Eddy there.

'Rosalyn.'

The sound of my name is jolting.

'Rosalyn.'

Part of me wants to keep staring out the window and hope that the annoying voice goes away but, unfortunately, I recognise it.

'Hello, Mr Cunningham.'

'Everything OK?'

I look at him as he stares down at me. He hasn't been able to find a seat, and he is standing, holding on to the hand grips. His tie has found its way over his shoulder. He looks like a man who has been running for the train.

I don't know what to reply.

It is typical of him not to be confrontational about my bolting out of his class.

'The next stop is mine, sir.'

'Mine too.'

Reluctantly, I stand beside him as we wait for the doors to open. Maybe I could wait for him to step off and just stay on the DART.

'After you,' he says politely.

There are quite a few people getting off at our stop, so I nearly manage to lose him in the crowd. But he is quicker on his feet than I appreciate.

'So do you want to explain to me what was going on in school today?'

'Not really, sir. I need to get home.'

'Well, you can either sit here and tell me or I'm walking home with you to chat to your parents.'

He sits down on a metal bench at the station.

Reluctantly I sit at the far end.

'It's slightly worrying, Rosalyn, when you teach someone for four years and suddenly they behave out of character. Is there anything you need to talk about?'

'I don't need to talk about anything, sir.'

'Well, delivering a speech and then running out the classroom door negates that statement, I'm afraid.'

He takes his tie off his shoulder and straightens it into place.

'Look, Rosalyn.'

'Ros.'

'OK, Ros. Do you prefer to be called that?'

'Yes.'

'Then you should tell the school, so that the teachers know.'

'Couldn't be bothered, sir.'

'But it does bother you, Ros. So, don't say you're not bothered. Do something about it. Care enough about your own feelings to support yourself.'

I take my phone from my pocket and pretend to read the screen, mostly to give myself time to think, but I just appear rude. However, Cunningham doesn't seem to care whether I talk or not.

'You see, Ros, to me it's plain. We have a class discussion on an unrelated topic, and you lose it over the fact that the school doesn't back the LBGTQ+ community. You say students are being moulded into gender stereotypes.'

'But we are, sir. Eamonn was right. Why can't Paddy Fitzgerald have long hair and earrings?'

Cunningham takes out his phone.

'Are you going to ring my parents, sir?'

'No, I want to show you this.'

He holds his phone out. There is a photo of a teenage boy dressed in tight jeans. The boy has long hair, and an equally long beard.

I look at the photo and look back at Cunningham.

'That's me,' he says. 'Fifth year in school. I was a rocker, Nirvana and Pearl Jam. You wouldn't think it now, would you? Even teachers need to look a certain way to teach. Private schools don't really like their teachers having dyed hair or a controversial appearance. It's an unwritten code. I suppose what I'm saying, Ros, is that none of us are who we seem and all of us conform to societal norms.'

I don't look at him, but I do reply to his argument. 'Are you trying to win me over, sir? Prove you're just like me and we have things in common.'

He smiles. 'It obviously isn't working.'

'No, it can't work, sir, because I don't know anyone like me.'

'And who are you then, Ros? Who's the real Ros Hughes?'

'If I told you that, sir, I'd have to kill you.'

'Good to see you haven't lost your sense of humour, even if you have lost your way in school.'

I turn to face him. 'I'm not going back to school, sir.'

'Is that wise?'

'I can't go back to school. Today was a shitshow.'

'Are you afraid to face your class?'

'I know what they'll think after my outburst today. They will assume I'm gay and nothing is further from the truth.'

Cunningham shrugs his shoulders. 'There's no shame in being gay, Rosalyn. Sorry, Ros.'

'Why? I suppose you're going to tell me you understand cos you're gay too?'

Cunningham, to be fair, has a great deal of patience.

'No, definitely not going to say that. And if you're not gay, what do you have to fear from your class? We can easily make up an excuse for your behaviour. Alien abduction maybe!'

'Banter won't work either, sir. I don't want to be rude, but I hate school.'

'"The brave man is not he who does not feel afraid but he who conquers that fear." Do you know who said that Ros?'

'No, sir,'

'It was Nelson Mandela.'

'Well, he was never transgender, sir.'

I hear the words coming out of my mouth, but I can't believe them. They are hanging in the air between us like dirty underwear. I am immediately ashamed that I have given them the light of day.

'Is that how you feel, Ros?'

'Sir, I'm going home now. I really don't want to talk any more.'

'Ros, have you told your parents?'

God, he's a teacher. He is duty bound to inform the school of any information that he deems could be a serious threat to my safety.

'I'm seventeen, sir. I don't have to tell my parents everything. And you don't have to tell them either.'

He is thinking. He doesn't reply immediately.

'I won't tell anybody right now. But will you promise me you will go to the school counsellor tomorrow and tell her what you've told me?'

'I'm not going to Ms McGlynn, sir.'

The idea of sitting in front of Dolly, with her mani-
cured nails, knitted cardigan and pleated skirt, makes me
want to stand back on my grandparents' garden wall and
consider jumping.

'It's either that or I will walk home with you now and
talk to your parents.'

My mind is spiralling, and I desperately look for an
escape route.

'OK, I will talk to someone, but not her.'

Cunningham visibly sighs and tries again.

'But she's the counsellor and she's very good at her job,
Ros. She will know the best way to help you through this.'

I shake my head.

'No sir. I can't.'

'Who will you talk to, then? Maybe you should tell
your parents?'

I look at him and suddenly an idea of how to contain
the situation appears. One that will keep the impact to a
minimum.

'I'll talk to you, sir.'

'No, no, that can't happen. I know nothing about the
problem you're going through.'

'It's not a problem, sir. It's who I am.'

'See! I'm really not the right person to talk to about
this.'

'You teach RE, sir, and you teach me English. I
trust you.'

He sighs. I imagine that he is sorry that he even talked to me on the train.

'OK. You can come and talk to me tomorrow at 1.40 in my room. But only as a first step. You will need to talk to the counsellor and your parents at some stage.'

I'm relieved. It's a stay of execution. I can string him along until next week and then he will have moved on to bigger school problems than me.

'But what about my leaving class today, sir? Won't I be in trouble with Viper? Sorry. I mean Mr Doherty.'

'I will talk to him in the morning and smooth it over. Don't worry about that.'

The evening is now pitch black and both of us are shivering from the cold.

'Go straight home, Ros.'

'I will, sir.'

'I am serious, straight home.'

'Again, sir, I'm seventeen. I'm not a child. I'll go home.'

6.30pm
Thursday
27 Beechfield Drive

The house is empty. Relieved, I go up to my bedroom and change into sweatpants and a hoodie. I think about taking the suitcase from under my bed and packing some clothes. I have relations in London. They could put me up for a while. And there are my grandparents in Mallorca. But I would have to explain why I was not in school. There would always be the need for an explanation.

Everything has gone into orbit recently. What was once carefully packed into the recesses of my mind, has spilled out since falling for Eddy. She has been the catalyst for my unravelling. But I don't want to be without her. I am true to the bigger part of me when I'm with her.

But what have I done?

Mr Cunningham, with his quiet ways, has proven my downfall. Him and his godly concern.

But his god is a god of the binary. The creator of Adam and Eve, and there is no mention of those who don't fit into those gender opposites. There is no mention of me. So maybe the Bible-thumpers are right. I shouldn't exist. I am an abomination of Satan.

I have looked it up often enough on the internet – searches on transsexualism and transgenderism. There are as many damning articles as there are supportive ones. And, get this, in Iran, gay people are sent for what we call gender-affirming surgery (I guess maybe they don't call it that) to purge them of the sin of being with another person of the same sex. The surgery brings them into line with binary behaviour. How weird is that? Maybe I should take a trip to Iran and get my surgery for free. (That is a joke. In poor taste, maybe, but I couldn't resist it.)

I can hear the front door opening downstairs and footsteps on the stairs. Before Mr Cunningham disturbed me on the DART, I had thought of this moment and what to say to her but, when my door swings open, I am lost for words.

My mother stands in the doorway, drenched from another downpour of winter rain.

'Is there any chance, Rosalyn, that what happened today in school is easily explained? Because I've had a difficult day and I'm tired.'

She shakes raindrops from her skirt and puts her hands theatrically on her hips.

'Why was it difficult, Mum?'

'No, don't do that, young lady. Just tell me why you left your English class today and bolted out of school.'

'Can we please do this tomorrow, Mum? I've had an awful day. I promise I will explain everything to you tomorrow. I'm meeting Mr Cunningham to apologise and discuss my behaviour. Maybe we could leave this until I talk to him?'

My mum looks at me suspiciously.

'I don't know, Rosalyn. All this is extremely odd of you. You have always been such an easy child. I can't understand what's come over you lately. Is it boy trouble?'

I feel a fraud when I force a few tears from my eyes and look down at the carpet.

'Oh, it is,' my mum says, answering herself. 'Please tell me you're not pregnant.'

'God, no, Mum. I would never sleep with a boy.'

A truthful comment amongst the lies.

'Then what is it, love?'

'I was dumped by my first boyfriend in class yesterday and I just …'

My mum is no longer standing over me. She is sitting on my bed, hugging me, and smiling.

'Oh, honey, there'll be many more boyfriends throughout your life. To be honest, I'm almost relieved. Your dad and I thought you might be gay. Not that there's anything wrong with that, of course, but it's such a difficult life path.'

I look at her, astonished. What the hell, even my parents have been questioning my sexuality.

When my mum leaves the room, I take my journal out of the bedside locker. I open it and write three words across the top of a new page.

STICK OR TWIST?

I put my pen down and look at the words. They conjure up memories. Summer holidays in a wet and windy Connemara, stuck inside the holiday home, pretending to have fun. Playing cards with Ian and my parents. Betting with matchsticks.

STICK OR TWIST?

I know what those words mean now. I am asking myself should I stick with being Rosalyn Hughes and stick with life as a female. Even go out with Paddy as my perfect cover.

Or should I twist, and become a male? Tell everyone my secret and let the cards fall where they may.

I write the word STICK down but immediately run a thick black line through it. I will never know my inner Noah if I STICK. Although I had decided not to go with that name. I could become Conor. A pretty innocuous name, but definitely male. Although maybe it has entered my head because it strangely resonates. I am a con artist, a conner! I have conned my way through life and, even if I have a so-called sex change, I will still be conning people. I wasn't born a hundred per cent male. My outer male will only be a fabrication of a doctor's operating room and a lifetime of hormone tablets.

But if I can't STICK, I must TWIST. What alternative is there?

I suppose I can give up the game altogether. Be like Plath and Hemingway? Would Eddy add me to her list of romantic suicides?

I think of my mum and Uncle Kenneth. There is no romanticism in his death. There is only pain. My mother and grandparents have lived with it for twenty years. I couldn't do that to them. It would be an act of desperation born purely out of a fear of facing my future.

> Hi. How are you feeling?
> Virus gone?

Paddy is texting me again.

> Much better thanks.

> That's good. Lenny died
> today. I'm sad

The straightforwardness of his message hits me. He doesn't know how to hide things and make them complicated.

> I'm really sorry, Paddy.
> That's awful.

> Thanks. She was quite old
> for a lizard. Twenty-five
> years. She once belonged
> to my mum.

> Oh no, that's horrible for you.

> Yes, it's losing another
> connection with her. Can
> we meet? I'd love a chat

> Of course

I can't say no to him. It would be cruel not to be there for him.

How about I pick you up at 7.30?

> You have a car?

No, I bought a sort of motorbike last week. My mum left me some money and I never spent it at the time

> Mum is never going to let me out with a guy on a motorbike!

Have you asked her?

> No

Then you don't know. She might surprise you

> OK. I'll ask.
> See you at 7.30.

> Great but where do you live?

I send him my address. Putting my phone down, I realise that my palms are sweating. Is this not STICKING rather than TWISTING? Why am I meeting him? I should text him back and tell him that my mother point-blank refuses.

But I can't. There is something about him that compels me to meet him. He is weirdly both old fashioned and radical.

I can feel my mother staring out from behind the curtains as I step on the back of the motorbike. And he was right about that too. It was a strange conversation with my mum. She had agreed without that much of an argument. In fact, without an argument at all.

'But if he broke it off with you in class,' she said, 'why does he want to see you now?'

'He wants to apologise, Mum. He says he's sorry. He was just angry at me for flirting with someone else at Tadhg's party.'

'You flirted with someone else when you were going out with someone? That's not nice, Rosalyn. I would expect more from you.'

'But I was a bit drunk, Mum. I acted like a real arse.'

'Don't use that vulgar language. Will you invite him in so I can meet him?'

'God, no, Mum, he would run a mile. He's very shy.'

'Well, please tell him to drive that motorbike carefully.'

'So, you're letting me go with him on his bike?'

'Look, I told you on New Year's Day that we all must live our lives rather than being afraid of them. If only my parents had let my brother live his, well, he might still be here.'

'But you don't blame Granny and Grandpa, do you, Mum?

She didn't answer that question. She just pushed me out the front door with a kiss on my cheek.

7.45pm
Thursday
A café

'Thanks for coming out.'

'I'm sorry your little lizard died.'

'Lenny.'

'Yes, Lenny,'

'Are you only here because you feel sorry for me, then?'

'Not really.'

I have suddenly found the moment to TWIST. Sitting in the small coffee shop with my sticky bun and mug of hot chocolate, I feel drawn to tell him the truth. Paddy is someone who deserves it.

'I am sorry you lost Lenny, but can I please talk to you about something?'

Paddy takes a sip of his drink and looks apprehensively at me.

'Nothing bad, I hope. I'm meeting you to cheer me up, you know.'

I shrug slightly and signal to the waitress for another drink.

'It's not a bad thing about you. You're actually a really lovely guy.'

'Ah, there's that word again – actually. You do know that you can't break it off with me because we're not going out together yet. But I'd like to go out with you.'

He is making what I want to tell him difficult to say.

'Look, Paddy, I'm not who you think I am.'

'Is any of us?'

I spoon the marshmallows from my hot chocolate on to the saucer and try again.

'I'm not a girl, Paddy.'

At first, I think he's going to laugh at me, but he just looks at me intently and says nothing.

'I've always wanted to be a boy. I've felt this way since I was a kid. I think I'm a transgender person. No, that's wrong. I know I'm transgender.'

He does something I don't expect then. He leans forward and hugs me. I can feel tears starting to run down my face. I feel relieved that I have told another person. When I told Mr Cunningham, it was a blurting out of a truth that I felt could destroy me. But this time it feels like sharing myself with someone I strangely trust.

'Well, that's a brush-off I didn't expect. And I thought I was a rebel,' he says, with a smile.

'You don't hate me, Paddy?'

'Why would I hate you?'

'Because I lied to you.'

He shakes his head emphatically. 'When did you lie to me? You've never told me you are a girl. You never told me anything about yourself. You were just a person in my class in school, and then at a bookshop and then at a party. Just a person being yourself.'

'But I lie by not telling people.'

'That's rubbish. None of us go around telling people who we are when we first meet. I didn't go up to you and tell you that I'm scared of elevators and monkeys and have an allergy to truffle.'

I laugh, even though tears are running down my face.

'Why scared of monkeys?'

'It's a long and horrifying story,' he replies. 'A trip to an animal sanctuary. I will tell you again some time.'

He puts his hand on my arm and keeps talking.

'It must be tough, not feeling right in your own body.'

'I hate my body.'

He looks sad for me.

'I can't pretend to understand how that feels, but it must be awful.'

'Thanks for being so understanding.'

He lets out a long breath. 'Life throws curve balls, doesn't it.'

'You really are so different from most guys our age.'

'Why are you always so derogatory about guys if you want to be one? I've told you before we're not all jocks and dick-heads. Is that the way you'd behave if you had a sex-change?'

He is talking about a sex-change as if it is the most obvious course for my life. It seems weird to have it normalised.

'No, of course not. I'd hope to be a guy like you.'

He laughs and shakes his head. 'You're already like me. We're both humans. Maybe the labelling should stop there. Then people wouldn't feel the need to escape gender stereotypes.'

I'm confused by what he's saying. I had never expected to get this sort of reply to my revelation.

'But I'm not escaping from a gender role. I *am* male.'

'Maleness is more than just a thought in our heads, Ros. It's a body type. It's anatomical.'

I can feel myself getting angry.

'I thought you understood. I thought you were a liberal thinker.'

He seems hurt by my attack. 'Hey, I do understand. You want to be male.'

'No, I *am* male!' My voice is raised now and the girl behind the counter looks over at our table.

'So have you thought seriously about having a sex change?'

'Of course.'

But I'm not telling the whole truth. I have thought of being in a male body and enjoying my life with Eddy as my girlfriend, but I haven't thought about the painful surgery that would get me there. I don't want to visualise how that would happen. The process scares me.

'But why did you kiss me last week?'

'I know. I'm sorry for that.'

'I'm not.'

'Even now.'

'Strangely, yes. Even now.'

'Does that mean you're bisexual? Because I've told you I'm male.'

'I don't know what that says about me. Why do I need a label? I suppose I just don't care what body people inhabit. I either like the person or I don't.'

I shake my head and move back in my chair.

'That's easy for you to say. You're happy being who you are. But it won't work for me. Every time someone calls me a good girl, I flinch. Every time someone looks at me like a girl, I get angry.'

'How does someone look at you like a girl?'

I'm irritated again. I don't want to defend how I feel. I just want to be accepted.

He notices my change in mood. 'I'm sorry, Ros. I shouldn't have questioned you.'

'It's fine. I question myself every day. I ask myself why I can't live in this body and be happy. But I can't. It just isn't me. And that's so difficult to explain. Can you imagine if you woke up in the morning, and looked in the mirror, and you had breasts? You'd be horrified. Well, that happens to me every day. I see myself a certain way and then the mirror shows me something entirely different.'

'That sounds hard.'

I'm struggling not to cry again.

'It is bloody hard.'

He has no answer to this. He just sits opposite me and drinks more of his coffee. I look at him and wish I knew how to explain myself better.

'Maybe I should take you home?' he suggests. 'Are you going to be OK?'

I nod. 'I'm sorry, Paddy. I came here tonight to help you over Lenny's death, and I've made it all about me.'

We don't talk much on the way out. It is another cold January night and we both want to escape the chilly air and the awkwardness that I have created.

'Will I see you again?' he asks.

'Why would you want to, Paddy?'

'Sometimes it's nice to have friends we can talk to.'

'I'll text you.'

1.40pm
Friday
Mr Cunningham's classroom

I knock on the door almost terrified that he will ask me to enter. I am hoping that he will have forgotten our meeting and will still be eating lunch in the canteen. Even coming into school today was a nightmare. I spent most of the morning arriving to classes late and leaving them early, hiding in the toilets between classes, avoiding conversations. But it seems like others feel the same way about me, as most people are giving me a wide berth too. Only Sarah has tried to talk to me.

I knock again, hoping he won't answer. But the door opens.

'Ah, Rosalyn. Sorry, Ros. Come in and sit down.'

He has reconfigured his classroom. The front row has been pushed back and a single chair has been placed in front of his desk.

'Look, I know you must be nervous about talking to me but it isn't too late to talk to the school counsellor instead. I won't be offended.'

I shake my head. 'No, sir, I'd prefer to talk to you.'

Although even the idea of talking to Mr Cunningham about my feelings makes me want to vomit.

'Did you talk to Mr Doherty, sir? Am I going to be punished?'

Cunningham raises an eyebrow.

'Let's just say he is going to give you the benefit of the doubt if I can convince you to behave in future. So, you need to convince me that you're not going to run for the hills again.'

'Thank you, sir.'

He nods, picks up a pencil and idly twirls it between his fingers.

'I read all about it last night, so at least our conversation can be real,' he continues. 'I didn't want to come in here today and show ignorance about how you feel. I've never actually met anyone transgender before.'

Having someone else acknowledge the secret I have hidden for so long is hugely discomfiting, as discomfiting as it was with Paddy. It is like having an embarrassing illness suddenly revealed.

No matter how long I have been seeing myself as a transgender person, his ease of discussing it is alarming.

'So how long have you felt this way, Ros? Do you want to have surgery? Is that the way you see your life progressing?'

It seems such an extreme idea – chopping bits off, taking hormones, watching my body change shape.

'To be honest, sir, I don't know.'

He looks at me earnestly and I have the distinct feeling that he doesn't know where to go with our conversation.

'Well, I can give you the names of a few groups that could help you, most of them right here in Dublin. They are very good and supportive. Have you heard of TENI, Transgender Equality Network Ireland?'

I nod. I had looked them up; but had chickened out from phoning them. I didn't want to make my situation real.

Last night I had faced the unknown with Paddy. But he had let me walk away from the coffee shop without any fears that it would lead to a whole new life. He didn't threaten to expose me or march me into a different world. But with Cunningham it now feels as if it's his job to get me safely into the world of a transgender person. I have become his mission.

'Or there's "Belong To". Any of these groups could give you support, and I am sure your parents will be supportive if you tell them.'

He is really going too fast for me. I don't want to tell anyone else, especially not my parents. They will think I'm making it up. How could their little girl be a boy?

I ask Mr Cunningham a question to deflect his line of thought.

'What do you think of transgender people?'

'It doesn't matter what I think, Ros. What matters is what you think.'

His answer irritates me. I don't want a platitude or a kick for touch. Because although asking him was a deflection, I do care what he thinks.

'No, I'm serious, sir. I want to know what you think. You're religious. You teach RE. Will I go to hell for being this way?'

He shakes his head emphatically. 'God, no, of course you won't go to hell. You've done nothing wrong being this way.'

'Then why does it feel so wrong?'

'Because our society is binary. We have been too closed to other ways of being.'

'But religious people like you think this is a punishable existence.'

He stops twirling his pen and places it down on the desk. 'Being an RE teacher doesn't mean I'm religious.'

'I'm sorry, sir. I thought you had to be religious to teach RE.'

Mr Cunningham laughs. 'Not at all. You just need to have a couple of free slots on your timetable. I have never been religious, Ros. Although I am spiritual.'

I don't understand him entirely because to me religion and spirituality are one and the same, both equally boring and also annoyingly present in your life. Like a dodgy uncle who keeps trying to tell you his life story at significant family dinners, always lurking in the background, trying to influence you with his narrow-minded views. And we can ignore him and pretend he doesn't exist, except he turns up at weddings and funerals, insisting on being heard.

'Is there a difference between religion and spirituality?' I ask.

I have tapped into his favourite topic. I can see it in his eyes. He is a passionate teacher, and this is his chance to lecture me on something he believes.

'A religious person follows a religion. But a spiritual person does not necessarily follow any one religion; he or she merely believes in the existence of spiritual things.'

'Such as?'

'I believe we all have a soul.'

'Oh, an atman,' I reply, happy to steer him away from further transgender conversations.

'Yes, exactly. And I thought you weren't listening in class.' He picks up his pen again and points it at me. 'Do you know, Ros, that your soul is neither male nor female? It is beyond all that. It is a blend of both, a union of all. It is part of the divine.'

'I didn't know that, sir.'

'And you are not your body, Ros. You are your soul. Your body is just the avatar of this one life. It is not the ultimate you. And we are incarnated in our present bodies for a purpose, Ros, and maybe you are in your body for a purpose. Have you ever thought of that?'

I shake my head.

He doesn't require a reply. He is now on a bigger mission than to help me become outwardly male. He wants to save my soul.

'This world has been locked into the masculine for centuries. The accruing of money, the conquering of peoples across the globe, the greedy multinational companies who devour land in their bid for more wealth – all this is the realm of unfettered masculine energy.'

Cunningham is now sounding like Eamonn and Paddy but just the 1.1 version.

'The masculine has been allowed to run amok. But the feminine is making a comeback, and it can't be allowed to run the world unbalanced either. We need the yin with the yang. And maybe people like you, who have both within them, can pave the way to a more balanced world.'

My face must register my disbelief as Cunningham gives me a small but decisive nod.

'People like you do have a part to play.'

'How can a transgender person like me make this dumbass world a better place?'

'Because you know the feminine, Ros, you have lived within a female body, but you also know the masculine, as your inner male exists. So you can teach us all how to bring back the balance of being both. The non-binary world is the key to our future survival.'

Mr Cunningham pauses for a moment.

I look at him aghast. He is mad. There is no other word for it. I have mentioned a transgender existence, and he is talking about avatars and symbolism and what sounds like complete fiction!

A bell echoes around the room.

'Is that the end of lunch? Look, good chat. We will have to continue this next week. That's unless you feel you can't manage until then. Because, Ros, I have to know that you won't do anything stupid, as otherwise we really will have to bring your parents in here. In fact, I may be breaking a few rules not doing that already, so I am totally trusting you with this.'

'No, sir, don't worry. I won't be doing anything stupid. My cup match is next Saturday. And you know me. I wouldn't want to miss that, sir.'

He smiles but not with a great deal of conviction. I can see he is wavering, so I quickly say goodbye and leave the room.

11.30am
Sunday
Bullock Harbour

The waves are crashing on to the rocks, spraying our faces.

'I really meant a drive up the mountains and a picnic on some grass,' Eddy says.

'But this is beautiful and wild and romantic too,' I suggest.

'Good thing I like you so much or I'd be off in my car.'

She kisses my cheek.

'Huh, your face is really salty from the water.'

We are not sitting at the front of Bullock harbour. We have walked through the concrete doorway and down the back. Climbing up the rocks has taken us to a completely isolated area, a place where we can hold hands and kiss.

'It's bloody freezing, Ros.'

'Then come even closer and we can keep each other warm.'

She snuggles up and places another kiss on my cheek.

What she says next stuns me. 'Are you going to break up with me, Ros? Am I too old for you? Or do you just prefer boys?'

My face drops. I can feel it happen. I know my mouth is hanging open in shock.

'I know we never said we were exclusive, but I didn't think you were into guys. Although, to be honest, we haven't talked about it that much. But you've never owned being a lesbian.'

I look at Eddy's face as if staring at her will give me some clue into what she is thinking.

'Why are you coming out with all this?'

'New Year's Eve. That's why,' she replies.

'When I was drunk?'

'When you were kissing a guy.'

'Why didn't you say something before, Eddy?'

'I was waiting to see if you'd tell me.'

I am unravelling. I feel our relationship is dying before my eyes.

'I came home from my night with Maisie, and I did what I said I'd do. I went looking for you. And I wish I hadn't. I found you with Paddy. I didn't know his name at the time. I had to ask Tadhg.'

'I'm so sorry, Eddy. I'm really so sorry. It was a mistake.'

'You seemed to be enjoying the mistake.'

'I was drunk.'

She takes a deep breath and turns her head away from me.

'Why didn't you say something that night, Eddy? Why weren't you angry with me then?'

She is looking out to sea, her eyes fixed on the horizon.

'I suppose I wanted to believe it was just a drunken mistake. And we never said that we were exclusive. But I suppose I thought it was something we didn't need to say. I thought you liked me as much as I liked you. And I also didn't think you were into guys.'

'But I do like you, Eddy. I love you.'

She looks at me with tears in her eyes and I feel anguish that I have hurt her.

'Are you bisexual, Ros? Or do you just prefer boys and I was an experiment? Because I know who I am, and I want to be with a girl.'

'God, you're not an experiment. I only want to be with girls too. I can promise you that with all my heart. It was just I never thought it would happen for me. I thought being with a girl was something that would only happen in my dreams. I never thought one would fancy me. I was prepared for a normal life or a life without dating at all.'

She is facing me again.

'What we have is normal, Ros. You sound so bloody homophobic. Do you like him?'

Although she is older than me, she seems younger and more vulnerable now.

'I do like him. He's a nice guy. But I don't like him like that. I was just scared of us. Scared where it would take me. Scared of who I'd have to become.'

'I was right,' she says. 'You don't want to be a lesbian. You think it's wrong.'

I stand up from the cold rocks and start to walk away.

'God, Ros, don't walk off. Don't be so childish. Finish this conversation and be honest with yourself for once.'

I stay standing, almost looming over her.

'I was just drunk and childish, Eddy.'

'And ashamed of being in a lesbian relationship.'

I shake my head. 'You have it wrong, Eddy. I'm not ashamed of you and me. I am just not lesbian – or bisexual.'

Eddy looks confused. She stands up and takes my hand. 'I don't understand, Ros. What are you saying?'

But I can't face this now. Standing in the cold with the spray hitting my face, I can't deal with all the emotions.

'I promise I will explain it, but please not now. I'm cold, and I'm embarrassed and I'm ashamed. I can't do more emotion.'

She accepts my stay of execution, but she needs reassurance.

'Do you still want to be with me, Ros?'

I'm not a singer, but I can repeat the lyrics off by heart as I've read them so often.

The first time I met you I knew you were the one,
I held you in my arms and my life truly begun,
We laughed and we danced, and we sang listening
to rain,
And I never want to be without you, Eddy, again.
Dance with me, dance with me,
Let me be the one.
Dance with me, dance with me,
Until our life is done.

She smiles at my rendition of her lyrics.

I kiss her cheek. 'I know I've messed up,' I say. 'But I really do want to be with you.'

She kisses my lips. 'No more drunken lapses of behaviour?'

'It will be my New Year's resolution – no more alcohol.'

She puts her head on my shoulder. 'Ros, can we please go somewhere warm now?'

'We can go to my grandparents' house. It's only around the corner.'

2pm
Sunday
Sandycove

'I like this house.' Eddy is standing by the window in her creased white shirt. She looks more beautiful than ever. She seems to have forgiven me. 'Being here I always feel like I am in some old black-and-white movie.'

She comes back to bed and slips under the sheets.

'What's your favourite film?' she asks.

'That's a difficult one, but probably *Avatar*. The first one, though. I saw it over Christmas with my parents.'

She moves closer to me and places an arm across my chest. 'Why do you like it?'

'I like action movies, but I also felt for the character.'

'Which character – the girl or the guy?'

'The guy. It was the fact that he fell in love with someone knowing he was not who he pretended to be. She fell in love with his avatar. It wasn't him at all. And he was afraid of showing her the real man in case she rejected him.'

Eddy fires another question at me. 'But aren't we all just avatars?' she asks.

'What do you mean?'

'You know, the idea that we are not our bodies, that we are so much more. We are a soul that just inhabits the body for one lifetime. Maybe your soul and mine have been in other lifetimes together.'

'As husband and wife?'

'Maybe, but maybe as mother and daughter, sisters, brothers even.'

'So you're not a good Catholic? You believe in re-incarnation?'

She looks at me with amusement. 'Don't you? I thought most people did these days. Heaven seems to have become redundant. Beliefs have become a pick and mix, haven't they? Unless you're one of those raging fundamentalists.'

I don't answer her straight away.

My world with Eddy is surreal. I have never talked religion or beliefs with friends before. I'm too shallow and generally uneducated, except for the snippets I can remember from Mr Cunningham's classes. But I like the idea of sharing past lives with Eddy. Maybe it's why we were so easy with each other when we first met.

'So do you believe in reincarnation, sweet thing?'

'I don't know what I believe in.'

We lie beside one another and say nothing more, as a shower of rain lashes the window. I love that she is lying in my arms. The male inside me is gloriously happy. If I could preserve this moment in time, then I would.

'My mum and dad made me sit through an old film once that was excruciatingly boring. It was my grand-parents' suggestion as an after-Christmas-dinner film. You know the one you all sit down to watch while con-suming a large box of chocolates, even though you're stuffed with turkey.'

'Which film?'

'I don't remember the name. I think I fell asleep too. They all thought it was thought-provoking and funny, but I couldn't cope with the fact that most of the film was the same event day after day.'

'*Groundhog Day* with Bill Murray.'

'That was it! I hated the film, but I would live today as my Groundhog Day, Eddy. Just spending this moment with you over and over again.'

Eddy smiles and squeezes my arm. 'That is the sweetest thing you have ever said. You're becoming romantic, Ros. But can I ask you something?'

I want to say no. I don't want anything to spoil this moment. But I acquiesce. 'Ask me anything.'

'I always get the feeling that you're holding something back. Sometimes we talk and you shut down conversations and move on to a different topic. Is there something you're keeping from me?'

My happiness is rocked by her question.

I say nothing.

'Because I really do feel that there is something you're not telling me. And you can tell me anything.'

I take my arm from under her head and roll over to face her.

'Let's just live in Groundhog Day,' I suggest.

'But there's nothing you can tell me that will upset me. We've got past that boy-kissing thing.'

'Have you really got over that?'

'I think so, Ros. I'm happy here with you.'

'Then let's leave it like that. There's nothing else.'

But she doesn't believe me. Maybe seeing me with Paddy has lost me that trust.

'I have done nothing else wrong,' I insist.

'Great. So tell me what's up with you? Because I know there's something.'

My hope of Groundhog Day is disappearing fast. But maybe I should lay all my cards on the table. Maybe I should TWIST not STICK. This may be my last chance of an honest future.

I have already told Paddy and Mr Cunningham and the world is still turning.

'It's like the film, Eddy. You love my avatar. This body is not who I am.'

'That's very deep, sweet thing, especially for you.'

I know her comment is not meant to offend. It's just part of our thing, to tease each other. But I sense she realises that this is not that type of moment.

'I'm sorry,' she adds, 'what do you mean? Although can I just say first that sometimes you seem much older than me. You're so serious. Maybe you're an old soul inside that body.'

Part of me just wants to kiss her and avoid the rest of this conversation. I want us to remain as we are. I want Groundhog Day.

'So, why are you not who I think you are, Ros? What's your avatar covering up?'

I look around my Uncle Kenneth's bedroom. I think of what my mum said a week ago, of him being afraid to be himself, to live his life openly. And now, all that remains of him are memories and books that my grandmother dusts a few times a year. I don't want to be like him. I don't want life to pass me by because I choked when the opportunity arose to be honest.

'Eddy, you are beautiful, you are funny, romantic and smart. I am so lucky that some idiot puked in your downstairs toilet, and I met you.'

She smiles. 'Yes, but I'm lucky too.'

'I don't want you to stop loving me.'

'You should be so lucky! Who says I love you!'

'Sorry. That was a stupid thing to say.'

'I'm teasing you, Ros. But I can't say those words yet, because that's a giant statement. And even my romanticism has a cautious side. I have already crossed some lines way too early with you. But I'm glad I have.'

She is making this difficult. She is so chatty and open, and I'm going to swallow it all back down if I can't spit it out.

'Eddy, I'm transgender.'

The room has stopped responding.

The rain doesn't seem to be hitting the window.

And the wind has stopped rattling the shutters.

Even her voice has ceased to answer me.

Time has stopped.

'Eddy, say something.'

Her quietness does nothing to ease my fears. But when

she speaks, she is not harsh or combative. 'I'm thinking, Ros. I'm thinking about what you've said.'

I look into her eyes to see if I can grasp an idea of what she thinks. I don't know what else to say. I just want to know what she thinks. I need her opinion on the stupidity that is my existence.

She sits up in the bed and pulls her knees up to her chin, wrapping herself into a protective ball.

'Transgender. So, you want to be a male?'

I'm relieved that she is still talking to me.

'Yes.'

'From a very young age?'

'Yes.'

'I don't know much about all this, Ros. I don't have any transsexual friends.'

'I'm not transsexual.'

'Yes, but you'd like to be, I presume.' She is over-simplifying, but she's trying. 'That's what transgender means, doesn't it? Someone who feels they are in the wrong body and wants to be in a body that reflects their inner gender.' She takes in a deep breath.

'Are you angry with me, Eddy?'

She shakes her head. 'No, not angry, Ros. Just confused. Why didn't you tell me before? Didn't you think it might be important?'

'I don't see why it really changes anything.'

She is looking at me intently now, as if to spot the difference in me.

'But it does change things. I'm a lesbian, Ros, and proud to be one. I want to be with another female. That's what lesbianism is.'

I can't reply to her statement. I feel like I have reached the top of a snakes and ladders board only to fall foul of the final snake. I am slithering all the way to the bottom again, trying to grasp hold of the sides as I descend.

'So, are you going to take hormones and have a sex change, change your name? What will you call yourself? Ross would do. Or will you be flamboyant and call yourself Roscoe?'

I am biting my lip. I don't want to cry. Not at this moment. Although I feel my tears forming.

It's not a masculine response to cry, which I know is gender stereotyping, but then if you are trying to prove to the world that you are a male inside a female body, you maybe have to go to the furthest end of the masculine spectrum to prove your point.

'So are you going to change?'

'I don't know. I want to be me. Male that is. But it seems such a frightening prospect, telling my parents, taking medication, having an operation.'

She is getting up from the bed now, putting on her clothes.

'I didn't realise how late it is, Ros. I'm sorry, but I need to get home. My parents want me to be there for dinner tonight. Some announcements they want to make. It seems like it's a day for those.'

It is the first time I have been with her that the conversation has disappeared between us. The gaping hole it leaves is airless and suffocating. Although she drives me home, she plays music to avoid any chance of words between us. Not the music we listen to when we're together but a discordant sound that I have never heard her play before. It seems more suited to Tadhg. It's heavy and aggressive. The journey to my parents' house seems to take longer than usual.

'Will I see you tomorrow, Eddy?'

'I have an essay to write. I'll text you.'

4.30pm
Sunday
27 Beechfield Drive

I can't face my parents. In fact, I can't face anything. My hand is clenched, and when I punch the mirror in my bedroom, the glass shatters into splinters, embedding themselves in my skin.

I hate you. I hate you. I hate you.

The words are internal, as most of my self-loathing tends to be.

I am so stupid. Why didn't I just keep my mouth shut? *We* were doing fine. So what if she doesn't know the real me?

Blood is dripping from my fingers to the floor. But I don't give a damn. I'm empty.

And maybe I'm wrong. Maybe she does know the real me. The person who hugs her, holds her, kisses her, is me. My body is not me.

She even said it herself. We are all avatars. None of us are our bodies. Cunningham said the same thing. We are souls clothed in bodies for a lifetime and then, when that lifetime ends, we will leave these outer cloaks and go back to source. Whatever that is!

If she knows we are more than our bodies, then why can't she understand that it doesn't matter what cloak I wear in this lifetime, it's still me. I don't know who or what I am any more. Everything is one chaotic mess.

I sit on my bed and now I am crying. In fact, I'm sobbing. There are floods of emotion leaking out of me. Maybe I should listen to everyone else. Maybe it doesn't matter what body I have on the outside. It's still me inside.

Crap. That's just not true. Our appearance is all we are in this world. People treat us for the bodies we inhabit. I am called a girl, and I hate that. If the world was only less gender-specific. If it was only less binary.

I look down at my hand. It is still clenched, and I am pushing splinters further into my skin. But the pain is inexplicably absent. My mind seems to have numbed my body, disengaged from it altogether.

Eddy.

Eddy.

Eddy.

I pull the largest splinter of mirror out of my thumb and jab it into my arm. But I don't even feel the usual pleasure of the pain.

I lie down on my bed and get under the quilt. If I can sleep, then maybe all this will go away.

When I wake up, I know I'm not alone. I can sense someone in the bedroom. Opening my eyes, I hope that I am back in Sandycove, with Eddy beside me in the bed and the rain still lashing the window.

'Jesus, Ros, what the hell have you done?'

Ian is the last person that I expect to see standing beside my bed, staring down at my bloody hand. He never comes into my bedroom. We keep a respectful distance from one another. He has his world and I have mine. It wasn't always that way. When we were little, we used to play together. We would build Lego castles and warships, bat caves and blanket dens. His friends were my friends. We'd run around on the green outside our house playing football. He didn't care that I was a girl. My gender was never mentioned. It never mattered. All that mattered was that I had a good left foot, and I was a wicked header of the ball. I was centre forward by the time we played in primary school.

In fact, I was happy until my body started changing shape and the boys started to notice. Suddenly, I went from being their friend to being another species. One that was to be kept at arm's length, preventing an interaction that could be seen as anything other than friendship.

'Ros, answer me, what's happened? You're bleeding.'

I look down at my hand. He's wrong. It has stopped bleeding, but it has covered the sheet and congealed into a mess between my fingers and down my wrist.

'I cut myself on the mirror. It fell and broke.'

'And you didn't think to get it cleaned up and bandaged? It looks a mess. What were you thinking?'

'Shut up, Ian. I don't want you here right now. Why are you in my room anyway?'

He looks worried about me. Something which rarely happens.

'Mum asked me to get you for dinner. But you wouldn't answer when I knocked.'

'Don't tell her about this. I can clean it up.'

He looks at me suspiciously. 'Tell her about what? The mirror fell, didn't it?'

My face obviously exposes the lie.

'Did you do this?'

I can't tell him. I don't want another trip to the counsellor, like the dreaded days of first year.

'Ros, come on, talk to me. Did you do this to the mirror?

But it doesn't matter anymore, everything is shattered.

'I smashed it. I lost my temper.'

He sucks in a deep breath and sits down on the side of my bed.

'Get lost, Ian, we're not that close.'

But he stays seated beside me.

'Is this about Eddy?'

'What?'

'She was in my class in school, Ros. We have friends in common.'

I turn to face the bedroom wall.

'It's not a problem, Ros. I don't care if you're a lesbian and neither will mum and dad.'

'Please go away.'

He puts his hand on my shoulder. 'Look, I know we are not as close as we used to be, but I do care about you. You're my little sister.'

'Then you don't fucking know me at all. So yes, we're not close.'

'Of course I know you. You're a pain in the arse of a sister.'

I turn to face him.

'Please don't say that.'

'OK. I'm sorry. You're not always annoying.'

But I shake my head. 'That's not what I mean. Don't say I'm your sister. I'm not.'

'Jesus, Ros, have you been smoking anything? I know Eddy is into it. Does she have you taking drugs?'

I push him from the bed. 'No. I'm not on anything.'

He puts his hands on his hips and looks down at me in confusion. 'Then, what are you talking about?'

'I should have been like you, Ian. I should have been a boy.'

His face shows even more confusion. 'What the hell do you mean?'

'Look at me, Ian. I'm not a girl. I'm a boy. I'm just stuck inside this pathetic body. While you have it all.'

He shakes his head. 'I don't see any boy, Ros. I just see you. And you're my sister. What's got into you?'

'Just leave my room. I don't want to say any more.'

He looks as if he wants to leave. He hates over-emotional outbursts. He's like my father in that way. But he stands there looking down at me, and realises this is not one of those moments he can run away from.

'Come on, Ros, what's really up? Cos that all sounds a bit bonkers.'

'I know it's bonkers. I've lived with it all my life. And sometimes I hate you for being who I want to be. I hate that I'm not your brother.'

It feels a relief that after all these years I can release some anger. A relief that someone in my family might be able to see who I am at last.

'Nah. Is this some kind of sick joke?'

'God, why is it so difficult to believe? I've never wanted to be a girl, Ian. Remember when we played football together and I was happy?'

'Lots of girls play football, Ros. Some of them professionally.'

'Get out, Ian. If you're not going to listen to me, get out!'

Neither of us has noticed but mum has entered the room. As she sees the shattered mirror on the floor and the blood on my bed, her face drops.

'What is going on here?'

Ian turns around quickly and gives her a reasonable answer.

'Ros's mirror broke, and she tried to pick up the glass and cut herself, she must have blanked out with the pain as I found her on the floor. I lifted her on to the bed. I was just about to come and get you.'

I look at Ian and he slightly nods at me. He wants me to back his version of events. However, my mother has moved into overdrive.

'Oh good lord, we must get you to A&E. Can you make it down to the car? Ian will you –'

'That's not necessary, Mum. It's only a few cuts and grazes. I'm not going to die.'

But my mother refuses to deal with me, I am now just her patient.

'Help her downstairs, Ian. I will wash it in the sink and see if it needs stitches.'

My father is sitting at the dinner table, waiting for someone to join him.

'Where have you all been? I'm hungry, you know. I've had a long day.'

'Oh stay quiet, Colin. Rosalyn has cut herself on a broken mirror. Just put the dinner in the oven to keep warm while I wash this blood off to see if it needs stitches.'

My dad leaps into action. 'You OK, darling?' he says, ruffling my hair.

I nod and try to smile at him. But I feel faint now. Faint and emotionally exhausted.

With very steady movements, my mother removes the splinters from my fingers.

'I don't understand how you got so many glass pieces embedded in your knuckles. I'm not too sure I can get all these out, some of them are deep.'

'The mirror fell, and I tried to catch it. I was just clumsy.'

'Not like you,' she replies, manoeuvring another fragment from my finger. 'I hope you don't have a hockey match soon, as you'll find putting your gloves on difficult. I suppose you're lucky it's Sunday.'

Dinner is a quiet affair. Nobody seems to feel like talking.

Mum has bandaged my hand and proclaimed that I won't die this time. It is something she has always said to us every time we have had a runny nose or fever. I asked her once why she said it. 'Oh,' she said, 'it's something your granny used to say to me, so I suppose it's just me copying her way of dealing with illness. She was very matter-of-fact and uncaring sometimes if you were feeling unwell. I hope you don't think I'm like that.'

Eating dinner is difficult. I feel like I am an inmate on death row, digesting his last supper. There is nothing to look forward to in my life now. It has all splintered.

'Mum, you know you told me the other night that I should live my life and not be afraid of being me?'

'What prompted that?' my dad asks my mum.

'Oh, it was just Kenneth's anniversary, and I was feeling emotional.'

My father nods and continues eating.

Ian is intently looking at me. He seems anxious, as if I may be taking a wrong turn.

'So why do you ask, Rosalyn?' my mum continues.

I glance at Ian. He is subtly shaking his head.

'Oh, no reason. A thought crossed my mind, but it's gone now.'

'Probably the effect of the strong painkillers I gave you,' she answers, patting my unbandaged hand.

I stand in Ian's doorway and look around his room. It is no different to mine. Male icons of film and sport decorate the walls, most going back to when he was much younger. Some of the teams and players we still support together – Liverpool and Irish rugby.

Ian hasn't noticed me in the doorway. He is scraping dried mud off the bottom of his rugby boots into a bin.

'Why didn't you want me to tell Mum and Dad?'

He flinches and looks up at me.

'I didn't think you knew what you were saying earlier. You can get a shock from nasty cuts like those. I didn't think you needed to add to the mistake, and I don't think you've thought it through, Ros.'

'How can you say that? I've thought of nothing but this all my life.'

He scrapes more caked mud into the bin.

'Is this a teenage fad, Ros? After all, everyone wants to be some gender variant these days. It's become a bloody trend to be different. Are you just looking for attention? You've always been jealous of me and how dad loves watching my games.'

I want to smack him in his arrogant face. 'Get over yourself, this is not about you and how Dad fawns over your rugby greatness.'

'What's it about then? You know if you tell Mum, it will destroy her. She only has one little girl and that's you.'

I pick up a book from his desk and throw it at him. It narrowly misses his face.

'What the hell, Rosalyn!'

He stands up from the bed and looms over me.

'I'm the son in this house. Look at you. Yes, you're strong, for a girl, but I'm the one over six foot. What kind of a male do you think you'd make at five foot nothing. Don't be ridiculous.'

I feel sick. I don't know how he can be so cruel. I don't understand why he can't accept who I am.

'Look in the mirror, Ros. You're a girl. You're my sister and whatever you say, you will always be Rosalyn to me.'

'But when you were in my bedroom you were nice to me. What was all that about?'

'You'd cut yourself. You were bleeding. I felt sorry for you. But not stupid enough to believe this bullshit.'

I don't know what to say to him. I'm shocked by his lack of understanding.

'Are you telling me that all transgender people are wrong?'

He looks at me as if I'm lacking in common sense. 'God, no. I'm not saying that. I'm just saying that you're not one. You've always been an attention-seeker. Look at your school refusal in first year, which just happened to be the year I was picked as captain of the JCT, and the year mum took up her job with the charity.'

I'm incensed by his suggestion. 'You don't know me at all.'

'Maybe I know you too much, better than you know yourself.'

'I'm going to tell Mum about me.'

'Go ahead, be selfish. And tell her that you've been sleeping with Eddy as well. That should make her happy.'

When I slam his bedroom door, the whole house seems to shake.

'What the hell is going on up there?'

'Nothing, Dad, just the wind slammed my door.'

7.30am
Monday
27 Beechfield Drive

I awake to terrible pain. My hand is on fire.

I turn off the alarm and look at my phone for messages. There are three.

> Hi, I think you're brave
> telling me what you did. I
> hope we can still be friends

I don't reply to Paddy.

> Hi, I messaged you
> yesterday. You OK? Sorry
> we didn't get to talk on
> Friday

I don't reply to Sarah either. I need to talk to her, but I don't have the energy for another questioning of my sanity.

The third message surprises me

> Were you being serious?
> Do you really believe
> you're transgender?

I didn't expect a message from Ian. Another beep comes through. Followed by two more in quick succession.

Look I'm sorry. I overreacted. You just shocked me.

Ros, I am sorry.

How's your hand?

I don't know what to reply. Part of me hates him. But I also want him to understand, to be on my side. I know he is sitting in his bed across the hallway, trying to reach out to me, but I am so hurt I don't want to even look at him.

His texts keep coming.

I am sorry.

I am here for you.

You're not alone.

> I know a friend who is transgender. I can introduce you. She's lovely.

> It was just difficult for me to hear something that I would never have guessed in a million years.

> I felt I didn't know you all of a sudden.

I wish he'd stop messaging. I don't want to forgive him for yesterday.

> You can tell Mum and Dad too. They would understand.

> I shouldn't have said that about being selfish.

> I was wrong.

The messaging disappears. I can hear his bedroom door close. *Please don't knock on my door. Just go to college and leave me alone.*

> I have to go to college now. I can be back before dinner.

> Don't do anything stupid. Like the mirror.

> I can get Cathy to talk to you. She'd really be happy to help. She went through all this.

> Have you told Eddy?

It's the only message that makes me want to reply.

> Yes

> That's good. I'm sure she'll help you too.

> She doesn't want to see me.

His messages stop coming. He probably doesn't know what to say to that. But my phone pings again a few minutes later.

> Ros, it will be OK.

> You don't know that, Ian

PART TWO
A New Construction

11.20am
Monday
Religious Education class

I am surprised that I'm in school today. I need the familiarity of something normal, but I also need to stay off the radar. But there is nowhere I can escape from the chaos now. I have wrecked every refuge, so I might as well be here.

Sarah has kept me a seat. She doesn't seem upset that I have left all her messages unanswered. I love her more for just being here without a barrage of questions. She is a rock – or trying to be one anyway.

'Today we will be looking into the ancient religion of Zoroastrianism. Which is a religion that may have influenced others, such as Christianity.'

There is a general groan around the classroom. It is only the eighth day back after the Christmas holidays and no-one is feeling the love for any religious learning.

'Less of the animosity. This is an interesting religion.'

'No religion is interesting,' Carl interjects. 'It's all boring.'

There is a general feeling of support for this statement.

Cunningham looks mildly defeated, as if he has also been struck by the January blues. 'So what would you prefer to talk about?' he asks, looking around the room.

'Can we just watch a video on something?' Rachel asks.

The rest of the Flock nod their head in agreement.

'That would be good, sir. Some rousing Ted Talk on how to make the world a better place.'

'Hell, no,' Carl snaps back. 'No more flipping Ted Talks. Why not a film?'

Cunningham rises from his seat and goes to a locked cupboard in the corner.

'You can watch a film as long as it has a spiritual theme.'

The class know this is as good as it gets.

'Fantastic sir, great idea.'

'I think the girls among you will enjoy this. It stars Brad Pitt.'

'He's old enough to be our dad,' Rachel says. 'You'd need a better-looking guy than that to make a religious film interesting.'

The Flock smirks.

'Fine. But at least it proves it's a Hollywood film.'

'What's it about, sir?'

'Wait and see. It's called *Seven Years in Tibet*.'

'I've seen it.'

'Shut up, Jessica.'

Jessica glares at the Flock and sits down further into her seat.

'Oi, none of that, please. Everyone has a right to their opinion in this classroom. Now move your chairs so you can see the screen and settle down or we will go back to Zoroastrianism.'

I don't care whether the film is good or bad. I can't concentrate on anything. I haven't heard from Eddy today. And I haven't texted her. I'm afraid to send anything in case she doesn't reply. That would be devastating. At least I can pretend that she is just busy, writing her essays.

I look up at the film and try not to think of Eddy.

But it is impossible.

When the bell rings, there is a general request that we finish the film in the next class. Mr Cunningham is not averse to the idea.

'If you're as quiet as today than maybe we can watch the rest. Now off you go and don't be late for your next class. Ros, will you stay behind, please?'

The class looks at me, wondering what I have done this time to gain his attention. Sarah squeezes my hand, but I shrug my shoulders. I have no idea why he is singling me out unless it's for another cringy conversation like the last one.

'Ros, take a seat,' he says when the others have left.

'I have politics class now, sir.'

'I will write you a note.'

There's a knock on the door.

'Shirley' Spencer walks in, nods towards Mr Cunningham and gives me a friendly smile.

'Hello, Ros.'

'Hello, Miss.'

Mr Cunningham holds a seat out for Ms Spencer and shows another chair to me.

The atmosphere in the room is making me anxious.

'Look, Ros, I told Ms McGlynn what you told me about before Christmas.'

'But, sir, you promised you wouldn't.'

Ms Spencer looks at Mr Cunningham questioningly.

'That's not exactly what I said, Ros. I told you that I wouldn't say anything for now. Teachers have a duty of care. We can't keep these things to ourselves.'

'Mr Cunningham is right, Ros. We must inform the relevant people of something major we have been told that can affect a child's wellbeing.'

I look at her angrily.

'Is that why you're here too, Miss, because you're my wellbeing teacher?'

Mr Cunningham doesn't give Ms Spencer time to answer.

'Ms Spencer is here because Ms McGlynn asked her to be here. Ms McGlynn, as you know, is retiring this year, and Ms Spencer will be taking over her job as counsellor. Ms McGlynn thought as you already knew Ms Spencer, you might find it easier to talk to her about your problem.'

I am more than angry now. 'I have told you before, sir, it's not a problem. It's just who I am. And you had no right to tell everyone.'

Mr Cunningham is uneasy with where this is going. He is not used to confrontation on an emotional level. He's one of the calm teachers, who bats all problems up to the hierarchy, and lets someone else take the pressure.

'Look, Ros, I know you're angry, but this is for the best. I'm going to leave you with Ms Spencer now and I hope in time you will see that this was the best option for you. I am not the man for the job. I'm not qualified.'

I don't reply, I just kick my bag on the floor and look away.

Shirley Spencer sighs at me as Mr Cunningham leaves the room.

'He's a nice person, you know. He didn't have much choice but to tell Ms McGlynn. He could be in serious trouble if he didn't. Surely you can understand his position.'

I don't want to listen to her bleat on about how difficult it was for him. I'm angry. I want all this contained. Even now, when my brother, Paddy and Eddy all know, I want it back in the box.

'Mr Cunningham says that you haven't told your parents yet. Is that right?'

'Do I have to talk to you, miss? I know he had to tell. But do I have to talk to you?'

Ms Spencer shakes her head. 'No, you don't. But what harm do you think it's going to do? Surely it would be nice to have someone to help you through all this?'

'But why should it be you, miss? What do you know about it? Neither you nor any other school counsellor knows what it's like to be me.'

'Then explain it to me.'

'Why? So you can tell me that I'm wrong or deluded?'

'Of course not. Why would anyone do that?'

'My brother did.'

She smiles at me in a supportive way. 'You've told your brother, that's good.'

'No, it wasn't. He was cruel. Told me I was pathetic and ridiculous, just looking for attention. And I'm sure that's what you think too.'

Ms Spencer moves from her seat and sits closer to me.

'I can assure you that's not what I think at all. Look, there's another reason why Ms McGlynn thought it best that I talk to you. My sister is trans. She used to be my brother.'

I look at her for confirmation. She nods at me and continues talking.

'She is three years living as a woman now. She is no longer the little brother I thought I had, and I am not going to lie, I do miss having a brother. But I love her too, just as much. And she's a much happier person than when she was male.'

'How old is she?'

'She's twenty-four. Eighteen when she first told us. But she should have told us earlier, she had already attempted suicide twice.'

'I'm sorry.'

'You've nothing to be sorry about, Ros.'

'I do. I'm sorry I was so rude earlier.'

She smiles at me which makes me feel worse.

'You are not to worry about my feelings, Ros. I'm a teacher. We're used to being the enemy. But I can help you through this if you let me. I wish someone had been able to help my sister when she was younger. She nearly didn't make it.'

It is strange how she is making me feel calmer. I do feel better talking to her.

'And I'm sure your brother regrets how he reacted when you told him. But it is a huge thing to absorb. He's probably just confused. I know I was when Alison first told me. In fact, I was a complete brat. Threw all my toys out of the cot, so to speak. I was only thinking of me of course. People always do. It takes them a while to get out of their own way.'

'Do you get on well now?'

'Aye, surely, we're the best of friends. We even go shopping for clothes together. She's got better taste than me.'

'Ian has already apologised.'

'Is that your brother?'

I nod. 'But he really lost it with me at first.'

'But he's apologised now, so you can move on from here.'

'He says he has a friend who is transgender and I can talk to her.'

'You see, you're not in this alone. There are loads of people like you coming out these days. There's lots of help out there.'

There is a weird unravelling of knots happening. As Shirley Spencer talks through all the avenues open to me, I can feel my stomach start to ease, and the fabric of the classroom changing around me. I have been in this school for over three years, and it looks different now. Don't ask me to explain how, but it just doesn't seem so confining. Walls that were once a mental prison are just concrete bricks painted white, and I feel I can smash through them and escape.

'So do you think you will tell your parents soon?'

The knots come back as quickly as they had left, and I scratch my arm abstractedly.

Ms Spencer puts a supportive hand on mine.

'I know it's easier telling people like me than those you love, Ros. I hardly know you. You have no history with me, and I have no dreams of how our lives will play out together. For siblings and parents, there are whole episodes of life with you that they will now see differently. But that doesn't mean that they will refuse to support you. Sometimes they just need time. Besides your brother, have you told anyone else, like a friend?'

I don't know whether to tell her about Eddy. I have opened the door to all this and allowed the truth to exist, but do I just keep going until every detail is divulged? Do I purge myself completely and raze my whole world to the ground and just begin again? It's STICK or TWIST time once more.

'I've told someone really important to me.'

Ms Spencer nods.

I'm relieved that she is not Ms McGlynn. Ms McGlynn would have been like talking to my grandmother, brusque and old-fashioned. At least I imagine her that way. It's easier for younger teachers to understand. They have grown up in a world where transgender children exist. My grandparents, even my parents, have such limited ideas of gender. But then why does Eddy not understand me? Why did she get so distant? She is supposed to be part of a new generation that sees past all these things.

'I told my girlfriend.'

The slight raising of an eyebrow tells me that Ms Spencer is surprised by that revelation.

'How did she react?'

I start scratching my arm again. I wish I could stop doing it, but the aggression has become a part of how I respond to things.

'She isn't talking to me. She doesn't want to be with a wannabe male. She's a lesbian and wants to be with a female.'

'She has probably fought hard to live her own sexuality, and having the goalpost change with your revelation is maybe scary for her. People your age can find all this so difficult to deal with. After all, it happens when so much is going on for you – the end of puberty, huge body changes, mood swings, an overall heightening of emotions. I remember being a teenager in school, it's tough. Let alone having to deal with a difference in your sexuality or gender.'

'But she isn't my age. She's in university.'

The eyebrow rises again, further this time.

'Well, if it helps, Ros, I wasn't much better when I was in college. I was still very raw and unfinished as a person. Just because she's a bit older than you doesn't mean she has all the answers. Maybe she just needs time to get her head around it. Sometimes when people have a secret they have kept for years, they can be so relieved to finally have it out in the open that they expect others to be as relieved as they are themselves, when they know the truth. But in fact, other people need to play catch-up. So, give her some time. You have had years to come to terms with who you are. Surely you can give her a few weeks?'

'Will my parents be the same?'

'Probably. They will try not to be upset. They will try to be supportive, but they will have had a part of their family life suddenly redefined. It's good if you can see it from their point of view. You need to understand how it impacts on those you tell so that you can be patient too. I hope you understand, Ros. Because if you can see it from their viewpoint, it will hurt much less when they don't react the way you need. Be prepared for some bumps in the road. But remember it doesn't mean they don't love you or won't support you.'

In everything I had ever thought about it, I had never considered exactly how it would make anybody else feel. I was always more concerned about whether they would believe me or not, and whether they would accept me.

'Can you be there when I tell them?'

She pauses and twists a ring around her finger.

'Do you want to tell them here in school? Wouldn't it be easier for them to find out in the comfort of their own home?

'If it's in front of you, miss, they can't react badly.'

'Have more faith in them, Ros. They may surprise you – in a good way.'

A bell rings in the corridor outside the classroom.

'Mr Cunningham will need his room back now, Ros. But I don't want to leave the conversation here. Why don't I ask Ms McGlynn if I can borrow her office later today and we can continue this. Would that be OK with you? Or would you prefer to find a room somewhere now? I'm free next class too.'

'I don't mind, miss.'

The door to the room opens and a stream of first years push through. Ms Spencer quickly turns to face them.

'Hey, you lot, out you get. You know you're not allowed into a room until your teacher arrives.'

'But the door was open, miss.'

'It doesn't matter. Out you get.'

The incoming mass of students exits the room reluctantly.

'Shall we meet later today? You should get some lunch and maybe have a break from all this seriousness. Are you feeling OK to do that?'

'We don't need to meet, miss. I'm fine, I really am. This has helped.'

'No. Let's keep it going, Ros. We have much more to talk about. And surely you don't want Ms McGlynn to think I've failed in my duty of care?'

'No, miss.'

'Then we can meet later. I'll send for you from class at twenty past three.'

12.40pm
Monday
The prop room

The room is as toasty as it was the last time. I sit on the floor with my back to the pipes and allow the warmth to spread through my body.

I feel strange.

I feel something I have not felt for a long time.

I feel hope.

Even with Eddy, there was always a fear behind everything – a fear of being found out, a fear of being dumped, a fear of telling her. Loving her was not enough to give me peace of mind. I was always living in the shadow of my transgender nature.

Maybe Shirley Spencer is right. I need to give everyone time to understand who I am. It is not something I can just dump at their door and expect them to immediately accept.

I wish Eddy would accept me. I miss her. But as much as I miss her, I'm relieved that there are no more fears to face with her. She will either take me back or reject me, but at least it will be me she rejects and not some pretend version of myself.

The prop room is eerily quiet. The hanging clothes look like an army of down-and-outs, standing in line for a free meal. I'm not here because I'm running away this time. I'm here because I just need the space to sit and think. And since it is lunchtime, no one will miss me. The school is big enough that I can easily say that I was somewhere else – walking the pitches, in the library, up at the music rooms. And Sarah won't be missing me as she has her debating group on Monday at lunchtime.

I should tell her.

My phone pings in my pocket.

It's Paddy.

> I've had an idea

>> What idea?

> Tut tut, you're on your phone in school

>> It's lunchtime.

> If you're going to change gender, you can call yourself Lenny!

I look at the phone and wonder am I misreading the message.

>> Lenny?!?!?!

>> Like your lizard!?!?

Yes

Why would I do that?

Lizards shed their skin
and you are going to shed
yours and start again

Bloody eejit! That's so
lame. Anyway I might not
change.

Really????????

I never said I was going to
have surgery.

But you will?

I don't know.

If you do we could be
mates!

He is the strangest person I have ever met but he is funny
and kind.

Would that not be
strange? We've kissed!

> Nah, we'd just be friends
> that have lost their benefits
> as I'm not gay

He makes me laugh. I am sitting in the prop room, properly laughing. He is the normality I need. He is not making it feel extremely serious or strange. He is making it feel acceptable and I love him for it.

> I talked to a school
> counsellor today.

> Did it help?

> Yes

> Well that's good

> I need to tell you
> something.

> Fire away

> I have a girlfriend.
> Or at least I did.

The return message is slower arriving.

Anyone I know?

Tadhg's sister.

Wow, didn't see that coming. When did it end?

When I told her about me.

The return message is slow again.

That's tough

Do you still want to be with her?

I don't know any more. I want to be me and she doesn't accept me.

Give her time. It took me a few days to get over kissing a guy!

I smile at the thought. Ms Spencer was right. There are so many ways that this impacts on others that I had failed to think about.

I'd kiss you again.

That surprises me. I don't know what to reply.

Does that shock you?

A bit. I've told you who I am. Does that not matter? And you just said, you're not gay.

His return message is slow. He's obviously thinking.

I know. It's strange for me too. But I'm sorry I still can't think of you as a guy. Your just Ros.

His message annoys me slightly.

You would if you could see the real me underneath this body. That's the problem. I'm stuck inside a shell that isn't me.

Who am I talking
to now, then?

What do you mean?

Who is texting me?

Paddy, this is too
philosophical for me. I'm
telling people my truth. I
don't need you to screw
that up.

Sorry

Lunch is nearly over. I have
to go.

Talk again?

Sure

I put my phone in my pocket.

He is the most infuriating person at one level. He picks
at things and wants answers that most people don't look
for. He sees levels where I see none. I exist in a black-

and-white world whereas he exists in Technicolor. Leaving school, educating himself, reading biographies on Victorian women, wearing long coats, and owning a full beard, he just oozes extremism. He pushes boundaries and jumps out of them, whereas I want to exist within them.

I don't want to be different. Paddy does. He would hate to be the same as everyone else. Moulded. Indoctrinated. Compliant. But I just want to be like everyone else. I want to fit into the binary world of male and female that is everywhere around me. Because there isn't a place or space for being both.

Damn Paddy. I wish he'd keep his thoughts to himself.

5.30pm
Monday
27 Beechfield Drive

Ian isn't home yet. I'm relieved. I know he wants to talk to me and be supportive, but I'm all talked out.

My second session with Ms Spencer was exhausting. She had so many pamphlets to give me. Pamphlets with circled telephone numbers, suggesting support.

My secret is out now and becoming a fast-moving train. Moving too fast for me to take a breath. But it is exciting and exhilarating at the same time.

I open my journal and write one name at the top of the page. I never know what I'm going to write until the pen starts moving. It's something I learned to do when I was at counselling for school refusal – stream-of-consciousness writing. 'Just allow the words to flow on to the page, Rosalyn, you will be surprised what comes out of your subconsciousness.' Surprise is often an understatement of the emotion I feel when I see the words on the page. Shock would be more applicable.

I look at my page now and the single capitalised name stares back at me.

LENNY

Shedding my skin and becoming another person is no longer a dream. Shirley Spencer had confirmed this in our meeting. 'This can happen, Ros. And here at the school we can support you in any way you wish – name change, pronoun change. Everything is set up here to help a transgender student. I know we haven't had one before, but it doesn't mean we're not ready for this.'

I had felt safe talking to her, sitting in the office with the low January sun streaming through the window. Everything appeared lighter. It was good not to be on my own any more. Someone was listening to me, understanding me, helping me.

'Thank you, Ms Spencer,' I said, 'but I don't know what I want to do yet. Coming out is one thing, having a name change and all the rest is a step further.'

She had leaned forward and offered me a biscuit at that point, as if doing something as simple as eating a digestive might bring us both back to the reality of where we are and what we are talking about.

'That's fine, Ros. You can take it one step at a time. There's no rush. But you do need to tell your parents, as it would be good for you to have the support of your family. And you should think of seeing a psychiatrist in the future, especially if you want surgery paid for by the state.'

That wasn't something I wanted to hear. What if a psychiatrist interviewed me and doubted the validity of my argument? I could just hear it: 'I'm sorry, Miss Hughes, but I don't think you're a transgender person at all. In fact, I believe you are merely deluded and possibly psychotic.' I know there is a male inside of me dying to be seen, aching to be acknowledged, but what will happen to me if a psychiatrist refuses to agree with me? Maybe the doctor will be like Paddy and Mr Cunningham and try to confuse me with spiritual ideas and philosophical arguments on what makes us who we are. I can't deal with those. I need clarity. Not more questions.

Ms Spencer hadn't confused me. She has a sister who was once her brother. She understood that not everyone is happy in their own bodies and not everyone can identify with their gender of birth. She told me how liberating it was for her sister to finally show that side of herself. The side hidden for years.

Ms Spencer understands how people think there are only two ways of being – male or female, Adam or Eve. And she understands that I am not an Eve. I have never been an Eve. And I know I am different from every Eve that I have ever met. So I have to be an Adam – right? If I'm not female, then I must be male. There isn't anything else to be, is there, in a binary world?

But Mr Cunningham had talked about something else – the non-binary. Those who feel neither male nor female. Am I one of those? How can I tell? I wish there were a test that could be administered to give the definitive answer to these questions. 'Ros Hughes, we have taken blood samples and DNA and we can confirm that you are indeed a male. Your body is an unfortunate accident.'

Right now, I am an accidental female. And remaining female is unacceptable. It is only my outer skin. My physicality.

But if Mr Cunningham and RE have taught me anything, I know the spiritually-minded would question this. Am I an accident or was I supposed to be this way?

I throw my biro against the bedroom wall. Mr Cunningham has infected me. I am caught up in all his ideas. I need to go back to the simple. I need to stick to the obvious: I am not Rosalyn Hughes, and I will never accept her as me.

It's time to tell my parents. I love them, and I know that they love me. Surely telling them won't change this.

I pick up my phone from the bedside locker as it is pinging at me.

Hello sweet thing

My heart seems to stop momentarily.

Are you there, Ros?

Hesitantly I reply.

Hi

Can we meet?

I hesitate again. I have missed Eddy so much. Cried at night over the loss of her hugs and kisses. But I don't know whether I want to be further hurt, listening to her telling me that it's all over.

> Please, Ros.

> OK

> Thank you. I'm here, at your house.

Now my heart is racing. I can hear the doorbell downstairs. Quickly, I shout down.

'It's OK, Mum. I'll get it. It's a friend for me.'

But it's too late. When I reach the top of the landing, my mother has already opened the door and is smiling at Eddy.

'Hello, I don't think we've met before.'

'Hello. Yes. Sorry to arrive uninvited but I just wanted a quick chat with Ros. I'm Eddy.'

'Hi, Eddy, won't you come in.'

My mother holds back the door and looks up the stairs towards me.

'Ros, you have a friend here.'

Coming down the stairs, I'm too slow to interrupt my mother's request.

'Would you like to stay for dinner, Eddy? It's only a curry but Ros rarely has friends around so it would be nice to hear from one of them.'

'That's very kind of you, Mrs Hughes, but I'm an awkward person to feed. I'm vegan.'

My mother regrettably takes the information in her stride.

'Oh, that's not a problem. I haven't put the chicken in the massaman sauce yet, I can leave some out for you and add some chickpeas. Do you like chickpeas?'

Eddy looks amused and embarrassed at the same time.

'Oh, please don't go to such an effort. I really don't need to stay.'

But my mother is turning towards the kitchen, with a determined look on her face. 'Nonsense. It's no effort at all. It will be nice to have something to talk about besides rugby and hockey.'

Eddy is standing in my bedroom, looking around the room.

'I cooked massaman curry once.'

'I'm sorry about all that with Mum. You don't have to stay.'

Eddy doesn't immediately reply. She is taking in every detail of my bedroom.

'It's you. Isn't it?'

'What do you mean?'

She picks up a magazine on rugby and holds it up to me.

'This whole room. It's all you. It's weird being here. It's like a window into your soul. It couldn't be more different from my room.'

I shrug my shoulders and sit on the bed.

'We're very different people.'

She doesn't sit on the bed beside me but pulls the chair from behind my desk.

'I hope you don't mind me coming here today. I just really needed to talk to you. I know I haven't been in contact, but I've been doing a lot of thinking. You rocked me the other day. I wasn't expecting it. It just came from nowhere for me.'

I don't want to talk to her about it. I just wish we were back in the house in Sandycove, with the wind-swept rain lashing the windows.

'To be honest, Ros, I'm angry with myself for how I reacted. I thought I was more liberal than that. I thought I was more open to things. But, do you know, I think it's because when I came out as gay it was such a big thing, and you telling me you weren't lesbian made me feel that being with you would be like abandoning my beliefs about myself. I have created a persona based on me being a lesbian. If I am with someone like you, then what does that make me?'

She stands up suddenly and walks towards the window.

'I don't know if I have explained this properly, Ros. Do you understand what I'm trying to say?'

But I don't know if I do understand it all. My mind is reeling.

She sits on the bed beside me and puts her hand on my arm. 'I miss you.'

I pull my hand away.

'How can you miss me, Eddy, if you don't even know me? You just miss the person you want me to be.'

She takes my hand back and shakes her head.

'That's not true, Ros. I miss you. It doesn't matter what label you give yourself or what label I gave you, you were still *you* with me.'

I heave a sigh and close my fingers around her hand.

'I hate all this, Eddy. I'm so bloody confused about everything. I wish I were normal. I wish I were a lesbian like you. But I'm not. And I know you only want to be with lesbians.'

She squeezes my hand and kisses me on the lips.

'Shakespeare says, "A rose by any other name would smell as sweet"' Your kisses are the same no matter what label you have. You did challenge me with your announcement. But I believe in soul mates, Ros.'

She closes her eyes briefly as if looking inside her head for the right words.

'And I suppose it's your soul that I like the most. And I should like that soul no matter what body you clothe it in, whether it's a male or a female exterior. What kind of liberal romanticist would I be if I pass up on love because someone dresses their soul in a different avatar? It should be what's inside the outer shell that matters. Shouldn't it?'

I look away from her, as there are tears in my eyes. But I can feel my body warm to her touch and my heart is pounding. I am excited that she is near me again but worried that she may not stay with me.

'The last few days, I have read a lot, sweet thing. It's my way of coping with things and finding answers. And the reading helped me. But to be honest, Ros, I'm still confused at one level too. I just want to go back to how we were. Before you told me.'

I smile at this. 'A Groundhog Day, then?'

'Yes, maybe. But I know that's not possible, and so do you.'

'I don't suppose you read anything positive about this. That helped you to think that we could still be together.'

'I might have. I read a wonderful line: "We need not think alike to love alike."'

'Who said that?'

'I can't remember. But it's very wise.'

Touching her hand, I want to give up on my future life in a male body. I want to pretend I am completely happy being the way I am now. But part of me knows that it won't work that way. Every time someone tells me I'm a good girl I will die slightly inside.

'But I can't be less than myself to be with you, Eddy. I've started all this now. I've told people. My brother knows. The school knows. And I'm going to tell my parents. I'm moving forward with this. I don't want to be with you if you can't support me being the real me.'

'I know that, sweet thing.'

She stands up from my bed and walks over to the window.

'I hate January, you know. It's so bleak, so cold.'

She turns to face me.

'If you still want to be together, I've decided to see where all this goes, Ros.'

'Really?'

She nods her head.

'Does that make me foolish, Ros? Maybe it does. And maybe I am not the one you should be with, as I don't know how I will react when faced with you becoming different on the outside. But I suppose we can try and find out together.'

My heart is hopeful now. She has not discarded me.

'I want to support you, Ros, and help you face the future. As Rumi wrote, "Goodbyes are only for those who love with their eyes. Because for those who love with their heart and soul there is no such thing as separation."'

I smile. 'I have no idea who Rumi is.'

'He was a Persian poet, my sweet thing.'

'We are really so different, Eddy.'

'I know.'

She walks over to my bed and lies down beside me. When she hugs me, I feel I have more than hope for the future, I have love. And when she sings, her voice fills my bedroom with more than the lyrics of her song.

The first time I met you I knew you were the one,
I held you in my arms and my life truly begun,
We laughed and we danced, and we sang listening to rain,
And I never want to be without you again.
Dance with me, dance with me,
Let me be the one.
Dance with me, dance with me, Ros,
Until our day is done.

ACKNOWLEDGEMENTS

I would like to thank everyone at Little Island for backing this book: Matthew Parkinson-Bennett who asked me to write a YA novel about a trans teenager, Siobhán Parkinson for her erudite editing and positive reaction, Kate McNamara for all her work on the publicity front and Elizabeth Goldrick who was the Art Editor. Little Island is a highly professional and supportive group of people, and I count myself very lucky to have become one of their authors and gained their expertise. I would also like to thank Jo Walker for her striking cover design.

Lastly a big thank you to my partner, family and friends who have always supported my writing.